"Get down!" Anna

She rushed at Jesse, trying to cover him with her body. She shoved him back inside the house. They toppled over each other, Jesse catching her before she hit the ground. She kicked the door closed with her foot.

Lying on top of him, she met his gaze, and her entire body shuddered with desire. "There's a shooter," she said, perhaps stating the obvious but feeling she needed to provide a reason she had tackled him.

He smelled good, like mint and earth. Realizing she was in an intimate position, chest to chest, thigh to thigh, she rolled to the side, moving off him.

She came to her feet and crouched by the front window to watch for movement in the distance or even catch a glimpse of the shooter. "Someone was shooting at me, bullets coming toward my car and your house."

Jesse left the room and came back with a rifle. She felt no danger from him, despite the anger in his eyes.

"I'll defend you," he said. "You have my word."

The Coltons of Texas: Finding love and buried family secrets in the Lone Star state...

Dear Reader,

Welcome back to Granite Gulch. Book four of this yearlong series introduces Annabel Colton, rookie cop and twin to Chris Colton. You'll have the opportunity to read Chris's book next month.

We have a lot of twists and turns waiting for you in this continuity: a serial killer on the loose, a father imprisoned, a long-lost sister, and clues leading to the location of the Colton children's beloved mother's body.

In addition to her family's struggles, Annabel is facing personal challenges. Her brothers don't support her career as a policewoman, and she is desperate to prove herself. Annabel meets Jesse Willard, half brother to the FBI's prime suspect in a string of serial killings across the county. She is assigned to stake out his farm in case the Alphabet Killer shows. The timing is wrong, the situation is wrong; everything is wrong except their chemistry.

I hope you enjoy this installment of The Coltons of Texas!

Best,

C.J. Miller

www.cj-miller.com

COLTON'S TEXAS STAKEOUT

C.J. Miller

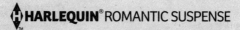
HARLEQUIN® ROMANTIC SUSPENSE

Special thanks and acknowledgment to C.J. Miller for her contribution to The Coltons of Texas miniseries.

ISBN-13: 978-0-373-27983-8

Colton's Texas Stakeout

Copyright © 2016 by Harlequin S.A.

Recycling programs
for this product may
not exist in your area.

Printed in U.S.A.

www.Harlequin.com

C.J. Miller loves to hear from her readers and can be contacted through her website: cj-miller.com. She lives in Maryland with her husband and three children. C.J. believes in first loves, second chances and happily ever after.

Books by C.J. Miller

Harlequin Romantic Suspense

The Coltons of Texas

Colton's Texas Stakeout

Hiding His Witness
Shielding the Suspect
Protecting His Princess
Traitorous Attraction
Under the Sheik's Protection
Colton Holiday Lockdown
Taken by the Con
Capturing the Huntsman

Conspiracy Against the Crown

The Secret King
Guarding His Royal Bride

Visit C.J.'s Author Profile page at Harlequin.com, or cj-miller.com, for more titles.

To my friend Amanda W. I am proud of all you've accomplished. The future holds many wonderful things! Thank you for your friendship and your fashion advice.

Chapter 1

Annabel Colton's thoughts veered off course at the sight of the handsome cowboy sauntering into the police precinct. Though he looked familiar, she couldn't place him as a resident of Granite Gulch, Texas. She would have remembered seeing the man of her dreams strutting around town. Granite Gulch was a small town, and having lived there all her life, Annabel knew almost everyone.

Just like almost everyone knew the Coltons. Not everything said about the Coltons was good but lately, mostly positive. Annabel considered that an accomplishment.

The sexy cowboy swaggered, confidence in spades, all six foot something moving through the precinct with determination and purpose. His blue-and-white plaid shirt covered broad shoulders, the sleeves rolled to the elbows; his worn jeans hung on him in just the right way, and he wore dusty boots, carrying his brown Stetson in his hand.

Annabel checked her mouth wasn't hanging open and averted her eyes to watch him in her peripheral vision. Her heart was hammering, and she felt dizzy. She took a deep breath. Women in Texas hadn't swooned in a century, and she wasn't bringing it back into style.

The sexy cowboy distraction took the edge off her frustration. She was working—rather marginally—on the biggest case to hit Granite Gulch in twenty years. A serial killer, nicknamed the Alphabet Killer, was stalking and killing women in and around Blackthorn County. The killer had taken the lives of six victims: Anna, Brittany, Celia, Daphne, Erica and Francie, in that order. The killer's obsession with the alphabet was one of their best leads in the case.

The police had been close to finding the Alphabet Killer, using clues Annabel had pieced together from reading the letters the killer had written to Matthew Colton.

Matthew Colton was Annabel's biological father, an incarcerated serial killer, dying of cancer with only a few months to live. His killing spree had ended in the death of Annabel's beloved, hardworking mother. Annabel's brother Ethan remembered seeing Saralee Colton's dead body in their farmhouse, a bull's-eye drawn on her forehead, but she hadn't been found. It was a source of great pain for Annabel and her siblings. Matthew Colton was dangling information in front of his children about where Saralee's body might be located. Like everything Matthew Colton did, he had an agenda. He did nothing for the sake of kindness, not even for his children.

The Alphabet Killer, who the police now believed was a woman named Regina Willard, was still free on the streets hunting for her next victim. If the killer stuck to her pattern, women whose names began with *G* were on the chopping block. The entire county was worried. This was the second time the town had been terrorized by a serial killer, and whispers and rumors about Matthew Colton and the similarities between the killers had been at an all-time high.

Annabel's curiosity grew when the cowboy stopped at her brother Sam Colton's desk. Sam, a detective for the Granite Gulch Police Department, and her oldest brother, Trevor, an FBI profiler, had been in deep discussion. They had not looped her into their conversations, likely centering around the Alphabet Killer. The extent of her involvement in the high-profile case had been to read the letters from Regina to Matthew Colton and provide what clues and interpretations she could. The Granite Gulch police chief, Jim Murray, had believed Annabel might have some insight, being a fresh graduate of the academy and known for her keen attention to detail. He had been right. She had pointed the FBI to the boardinghouse in Rosewood where Regina had been staying.

Sam and Trevor straightened as the cowboy spoke to them. Their body language was defensive, and after several exchanges, the three men looked ready to throw fists.

When her brothers led the man to the interrogation room, Annabel beelined for the observation deck. If Trevor and Sam wanted to speak to this man, then it had to be about the Alphabet Killer. She wanted to know how he was involved. Could they finally have a witness who could provide a solid lead?

Watching the man up close, Annabel confirmed her initial assessment. He was gorgeous. His blond hair was cut longer but kept neat, and his green eyes were piercing. She was glad he decided to sit facing the one-way mirror. She could read his expression and body language.

Given his clothes and build, he could work on any of the nearby farms or ranches and be new to the area. Her friend Mia was usually the first to know about any eligible bachelors who moved to Granite Gulch. Maybe this emerald-eyed cowboy was already taken and, thus, why Mia hadn't mentioned him. That would figure. All the best ones were.

Focusing on the conversation, Annabel turned on the listening speaker, hoping the pop didn't draw her brothers' attention. They wanted her uninvolved in the Alphabet Killer case, even though she had made an important contribution to it. She was a rookie on the force, and her brothers believed she needed to earn her chops before catching a real case.

The cowboy had laid his hat on the table in front of him. "I've been cooperative. I've answered your questions at length. Please, leave me and my employees alone. You're impacting my business, and I can't allow that to continue."

As his statements fell into context, Annabel placed him. Jesse Willard, brother to the prime suspect in the alphabet killings. Annabel had seen a photo of him in the case file as a person of interest in assisting Regina Willard. The police and FBI suspected Regina Willard had help hiding from and dodging the authorities, but they hadn't pinned down who exactly was assisting her. Her personal history was marred with failed relationships. Her parents were dead. But Regina had to have an ally to evade the police and FBI this long.

"We're trying to stop a murderer. We're not backing down from any leads until we find Regina," Sam said.

Trevor was watching the exchange with his dark, assessing gaze. Annabel didn't mistake his silence for disinterest. Trevor was analytical and intelligent. He was likely scrutinizing every movement, every eyebrow raise and every twitch of Jesse's hand.

According to the case notes and what Annabel had overheard around the precinct, Trevor had spoken to Jesse before, but Annabel could picture him waiting for Jesse to inadvertently give something away that would help them find Regina.

Jesse plowed a hand through his hair in frustration. "I've told you before. I am not hiding my sister. I haven't seen her in years."

"How do we know you'll come forward if you see her? What if she stops by your farm? Will you alert us?" Sam asked.

Jesse stared at Sam for a long moment, unblinking. His mouth twitched as if checking his words and trying to wrangle his temper under control. "While I am not convinced Regina has anything to do with these murders, if I saw her, I would let her know you wanted to speak with her. I'll even drive her here myself. I want to put this matter behind me. It's bad for business."

"We have undercover FBI agents and police officers across the state looking for Regina. She hasn't turned up. She's getting help from someone," Sam said. He folded his arms and looked pointedly at Jesse.

Annabel flinched, sensing Sam was pushing Jesse too hard. He had come to the police station on his own accord. If he was involved with a murderer, he would avoid the police. Something about his face and his body language told Annabel he was telling the truth about Regina, and that was disappointing. He didn't know where Regina was, and, therefore, they still didn't have a solid lead to follow.

That didn't mean Regina wouldn't turn up at Jesse's farm in the near future, but for now, Jesse wasn't hiding her.

"I can see I've wasted my time coming down here," Jesse said and stood to leave.

He wasn't under arrest, and they couldn't hold him and barrage him with questions. As he walked toward the door, Annabel shut off the speaker and hurried back toward the information desk. Her assignment was the dullest in the entire department, and she'd pretend she hadn't been listening to the conversation.

As she rounded the corner, she slammed into

Jesse and lost her balance. He smelled of earth and spices, a masculine, clean scent. He reached to steady her, grabbing her arm with his free hand, his Stetson in the other. His grip was strong and firm. Her heart fluttered as she lifted her gaze to meet his. As their eyes met, she was struck all over again by how devastatingly handsome he was and how his green eyes seemed to see into her soul. Electricity and heat snapped between them. Annabel didn't know she could feel this intensely for a man she hadn't exchanged one word with. Did Jesse feel it, too?

Her breasts brushed his hard chest, and she felt every nerve ending in her body come to attention. Long-slumbering desire roared awake. She was already imagining rubbing her body against his, kissing his perfect mouth and running her hands across his hard body.

"Excuse me," she said, her voice coming out breathy.

He nodded at her once swiftly. "Are you all right, ma'am?"

Nothing in his face gave away he was having the same dirty thoughts about her that she was about him. "I'm fine."

He released her arm, and she dropped her hand from the front of his shirt where she had been holding on to the fabric. It wasn't in her nature to play the damsel in distress, especially when she was in uniform, but something about him made her want to blush, bat her eyelashes and giggle.

"Have a good day," he said.

Why couldn't she think of something clever to say? Something to flirt with him, to convince him to stick around another few minutes? Flirting wasn't her forte, and in front of Jesse, she felt tongue-tied.

As he walked away, she turned to watch him leave, appreciating how his jeans hung low on the tilt of his hips and—

"Annabel."

She turned at the sound of her name. Sam was glaring at her. Trevor was assessing her. She set her hand on her hip, giving them as much sass as she could muster. "What?"

"What are you doing? Do you know who that man is?" Sam asked.

"Jesse Willard. Person of interest in an ongoing investigation," she said, feeling hot and bothered and trying to pretend to be unaffected by her run-in with Jesse. Could her brothers see on her face she was attracted to Jesse? It had been obvious to her, and she felt her brothers would be quick to pick up on changes in her expression or body language.

"Person of interest in a serial-killer investigation. Watch yourself," Sam said.

Though younger than her, Sam outranked her in the Granite Gulch Police Department. She wanted to shoot her mouth off and remind him that she was a police officer, she could handle herself, and she didn't need his warning. But she kept her mouth shut, knowing her rookie status combined with Sam's in with their boss, Chief Jim Murray, could mean she'd face another week of the world's most boring assignments. As it was, she was doomed to a morning of fielding nonimportant, nonemergency calls, like explaining to the town busybody why a couple's consensual, adult affair wasn't a matter for the police or why a missing cat didn't warrant a fire department, EMT and police response.

"Yes, sir," she said, keeping her mocking tone to a minimum. She loved her brothers, but they could be overprotective pains in her side.

She returned to the information desk, her body still buzzing from the contact with Jesse Willard. After answering the phones for three hours, her partner, Luis Gonzales, arrived. At least in the afternoon, she and Luis would work the streets, heading out in the squad car and responding to emergencies. Though her brother's influence in the GGPD meant she and Luis would catch the tamest emergency calls, anything was better than sitting at a desk all day.

Annabel had followed her dreams in becoming a police officer, and she hoped, with more hard work, it would be everything she'd imagined. She'd like to stop actual criminals, prevent crime and be a positive influence on the Granite Gulch community. While she alone couldn't repay the huge debt her father owed society for his crimes, Annabel felt better knowing she was doing her best.

Maybe someday soon, that would start to feel like enough.

Another farmhand hadn't shown up for work. Given the week he was having, Jesse Willard was in no mood to deal with additional problems the lack of help created. Longer hours and less sleep, the downsides of being the boss.

Owning a farm had been his dream, and it had its ups and downs. Lately, far more downs than ups.

Several important customers had cancelled their orders with him. They had hedged around the reason, but Jesse knew. He'd heard the rumors circulating in town that his sister—more specifically, his half sister—Regina was involved with the murders around Granite Gulch and nearby towns. Living in a small town meant the close-knit community led folks to believe everyone's business was their business. Jesse lived forty minutes from Main Street, and he kept his visits to town brief. He was polite but detached when the town busybodies circled him. He preferred to keep to himself, but rumors about Regina were persistent. The Alphabet Killer was big news, and he couldn't go a day without someone speculating on the reasons for the murders or the next victim.

Jesse didn't know why the police and FBI suspected Regina. His older sister was a little off, and she could be disagreeable, but that was a far cry from being a murderer. He suspected it was more guesswork than actual evidence involved. Regina wasn't capable of committing a murder, especially not a series of murders that were as methodical and cold as the media was describing.

Jesse had driven to the police station that morning, thinking the police would be reasonable. He'd thought they could talk man-to-man, but of course those Colton brothers thought they owned Granite Gulch. Their family tree had its share of nuts, but that didn't slow them down. They thought Regina was the murderer, and they were bent on proving it. Maybe they believed themselves experts because they'd lived through an ordeal with their father. The similarities in the cases, which the media were quick to point out, were disturbing.

Why were they investigating the case anyway? Weren't there serious conflicts of interest with the children of a serial killer investigating another serial killer, especially when the cases were connected?

It was another backward thing about Granite Gulch. It ran by its own rules. Add that to the reasons Jesse preferred to keep to himself.

Knowing he wasn't in the mood to talk to anyone, he headed to the barn. He needed to check his supplies and calculate what to order. Losing customers was rough when his profit margins were slim, but he'd find somewhere to cut extras from the budget.

Some days, he wished he hadn't bought this farm. He loved being his own boss and setting his own hours, but there was a freedom in working as a farmhand, migrating to a new place on a whim. Setting his own hours often meant working seven days a week to complete tasks, spending ten hours in the field and then handling bills and paperwork another two hours at night.

As he inventoried, Jesse's thoughts turned to the brunette he had run into that morning at the police precinct. In keeping with his luck, she had been wearing a police uniform. That should have turned him off immediately, but she filled it out nicely and it made him forget how much he detested the sight of the navy uniform in general. The brunette cop was trim and shapely, a woman who could get him going.

Her eyes were intelligent and trusting. She must not have been a cop long. The cops he knew were hard around the edges, having too many experiences with criminals and liars to see the good in people anymore. Most of Jesse's memories of the police from his childhood were bad: yelling and sweeping in without fixing the problem. When they'd left, it had always been worse.

Maybe the Coltons' jobs were making them cynical and eager to rush to judgment. They'd grown up with a serial killer for a father who'd murdered their mother. That had to have destroyed them. Who wouldn't be traumatized by a childhood of violence and loss and spending their careers with liars and criminals? Jesse knew firsthand exactly how hard it was to keep the past as ancient history and not let it creep into everyday life.

"Hey, Mr. Jesse!"

At the sound of Noah's voice, Jesse's bad mood lifted. Noah was the son of one of his farmhands and sometimes came with his mother to work. Noah liked talking to Jesse, and since he didn't cause trouble and his mother worked hard, Jesse didn't have complaints about him tagging along behind him. He'd actually grown accustomed to the boy's company and enjoyed listening to his stories.

"Did you hear the good news?" Noah asked.

Jesse could use some good news. "Nah, what did I miss?"

Sometimes, Noah's news was about his sixth grade class, which wasn't anything for Jesse to get excited about, but the boy needed to talk. Jesse hoped he could sometimes offer advice to keep Noah on the straight and narrow. He was a good kid, and, despite his father having left Noah and his mom before Noah was born, Noah didn't seem lacking in parental love.

Noah tipped his red ball cap back on his head. "Mom's having a baby."

Jesse stopped, unsure if he had misheard Noah. The boy was right behind him. He turned. "Your mother is pregnant?"

"That's what she said. It's a secret, though, so don't let it get around town."

Jesse tried to remember what tasks Grace had been assigned for the day. Monitoring the cows? She could get kicked in the stomach. Repairing fencing? That was heavy, hard work. Grace was an experienced farmhand. Should he approach her? Let her know he could give her modified assignments? Offer her leave from work? Jesse knew nothing about babies and even less about pregnancy. What was the right thing to do?

His conscience wouldn't rest easy until he spoke with Grace. As not to alarm Noah or make the boy think he had caused any problem, he set down his clipboard. "I'll be right back. Why don't you give me a hand and take that bag of duck feed to the pond?" It was a task Noah loved, and it had gotten to the point that, when the ducks saw Noah coming, they flocked toward him.

Noah grabbed the small bag of feed. "Okay. Be right back!"

Jesse checked the task schedule. Grace was assigned to the horses that day. He found Grace right where she should have been, feeding the horses. "Hey, Grace."

She jumped at the sound of her name and turned. "Hey, boss."

"Everything okay?" he asked. He didn't want to ask her directly in case she wasn't ready to talk about it.

Grace was smart. Lines formed around the corners of her eyes. "Noah told you." She sighed.

He didn't want the boy in trouble. "He cares about you and so do I. I can pretend not to know until you're ready to tell me. But I want you to know I have plenty of work that might be less taxing. But it's up to you, okay?"

Grace brushed her long brown bangs to the side. The rest of her hair was twisted on the back of her head and pinned. "The others will be upset if I'm given the easy work."

Jesse folded his arms. "There is nothing easy on this farm, and everyone knows it. Plus, I'm the boss. What I say goes. When Tom broke his arm last year in that car accident, no one said a thing when he was given work he could manage."

Grace's eyes filled with tears, and she hugged Jesse. "Thank you." After a couple seconds, she broke away and wiped at her eyes. "I've been tired and emotional. I was worried about telling you and the other guys. I don't want anyone to think I'm getting special treatment."

"If anyone has a problem with your work, tell them to speak to me. Got it?"

"Yes, boss," she said with a smile.

Jesse would leave it at that. He'd adjust the schedule going forward and keep Grace safe. Grace seemed to be unaware that Tom, his foreman, had a soft spot for Grace, and the other guys looked to Tom for guidance. Tom would be fine with whatever Grace did, and the other guys would follow his lead.

As Jesse walked back to the barn, he thought again of the brunette police officer. He didn't have a good reason to see her again. But maybe he'd go into town to buy a few fencing pliers to replace ones that had broken. If his path crossed with the police officer, it would be well worth the trip.

"Tough break in Rosewood," Luis said, adjusting the air-conditioning in the car. It was eighty-three degrees, and it felt hotter inside the vehicle.

Annabel set her iced coffee in the cruiser's cup holder. "Yeah." She didn't want to talk about it. Annabel had agreed to read the letters sent from Regina to Matthew, less as a police officer and more as a relation to Matthew Colton.

Though the police had been too late to catch Regina Willard, her room in Rosewood had convinced them that they had the right person. The walls in Regina's room had been covered in the alphabet, written in red permanent marker, a bull's-eye drawn beside each letter and newspaper articles of the victims posted on the walls. Hundreds of clippings, obsessive and disturbing. Regina used the same red marker and the bull's-eye on the foreheads of her victims after she killed them. "Regina's in the wind."

"We'll get another break," Luis said.

Regina was no longer writing to Matthew Colton in prison. They had the letters and not much else. The FBI might find something in her room or perhaps they'd receive a tip on their hotline, but the more time that passed, the colder the trail grew. "Hopefully soon."

"What letter is she up to? *G*?" Luis asked.

"G," Annabel confirmed. The Alphabet Killer, while adopting some of Matthew Colton's rituals, had added some of her own. She was killing women of a certain profile—long, dark hair, twenty to thirty-five years old—in letter order based on her victims' first names. The police hadn't caught the pattern until the killer's third victim, Celia Robison, had been killed on her wedding day. She'd had a bull's-eye center dot slightly off center to the left drawn on her forehead. Celia had been Sam's fiancée, and her death had brought the serial killer case even closer to home. So close, in fact, the FBI previously suspected Annabel's long-lost sister, Josie, of being the Alphabet Killer. Annabel was relieved the FBI had turned their attention away from Josie. No matter what rumors swirled

about Josie, Annabel wouldn't believe her missing sister was a killer.

They had their father's blood in them, undeniably, but each of Matthew Colton's children had chosen honorable and respectable jobs on the right side of the law. Though she couldn't know for sure, Annabel believed the same was true of Josie.

The car radio beeped. Annabel answered and waited for the message and code and tried not to let disappointment nip at her. They had to investigate a missing cat. Again. Annabel hid her annoyance and ignored Luis's grimace. He was an experienced cop, and before being paired with her, he'd worked much more interesting cases.

After Annabel acknowledged the code and location, Luis made a U-turn in the direction of the house with the missing cat. "You realize this is the same dingbat who lost her cat last week?" Luis asked.

"I realize it," Annabel said.

"Cat's probably hiding in her house again," Luis said. The last time Mrs. Granger had called them to help find her cat, Cubbles had been sleeping in a windowsill.

"She called us. We need to take it seriously," Annabel said.

"Fine, but I'm not turning on the lights and sirens for this," Luis said.

"I agree. But we will check the windowsill first," Annabel said.

This was a familiar discussion between them. Luis had much less patience for calls he considered a waste of police resources. Some of the calls seemed silly, but she was eager to prove herself. They had to respond to calls—even the ones that were a waste of her time. If she could get the chief and Sam to see her as more than a rookie in need of protecting, she might prove to them she was capable of actual police work.

Chapter 2

Ethan and Lizzie had invited the Colton siblings to their ranch house for dinner. Annabel didn't know how Lizzie was managing to cook dinner for so many people when she was due to have her baby soon. Most days after work, Annabel was so tired she heated dinner in the microwave and had a glass of wine.

Ethan and Lizzie were jazzed about their baby. It was almost hard to watch. They were in love, and after what they had been through, they deserved every moment of happiness they'd found together.

Of course, not all of the Colton siblings would be in attendance. Josie wanted nothing to do with her biological family. Despite Trevor's FBI resources, Sam's detective skills and Chris's PI abilities, they hadn't been able to locate her.

Annabel wondered what they had done, or hadn't done, to make Josie hate them. Lizzie had been in foster care with Josie, and she didn't recall Josie speaking angrily about her siblings. Annabel worried Josie had gotten herself into trouble, perhaps drug use or hanging with the wrong crowd. Given how the Colton siblings had grown up, the statistics weren't in their favor for them becoming successful and productive members of society. She and her brothers had worked hard in their careers, and Annabel believed her brothers carried the same burden of their father's crimes with them. Annabel thought Josie had risen above the past, but in dark moments of doubt, concerns plucked at her.

Annabel parked outside the ranch house. She was pleased to see her twin's white pickup truck in front of the house. Annabel could confide in Chris, and he didn't seem to resent her new career as a police officer as much as her other siblings. Whether it was because she and Chris had their twin connection or because they'd become and stayed close in high school, he listened to her. She could tell him anything.

Last year when Annabel had graduated from the police academy at the top of her class, she had thought her brothers would see her desire to be a police officer, and one day a detective, wasn't a whim or an act of defiance against them.

Only Sam had been present at her graduation, and that was because most of the current members of the GGPD attended the ceremony. Her brothers' absences had hurt her more than she'd ever said. They rarely asked her about her job, nor did they acknowledge her professional accomplishments. Annabel tried to remain calm about it and pretend she didn't care. Their family was facing enough problems, and her brothers wouldn't take kindly to criticism.

Taking a deep breath and focusing on the reason she was there, to see her family and discuss the clues Matthew Colton had provided them, Annabel rang the doorbell.

Sam answered, beer in hand, and he greeted her with a hug. At least when they were at family gatherings, he didn't act like her superior. He was a detective, and she, six years older, was a rookie cop. His frostiness at work was his way of keeping her away from dangerous cases, as if that would keep her safe. Random, bad things happened all the time, even to cops who were assigned missing-cat reports.

She lived with that knowledge and had since the day her mother had been murdered. Annabel's soul wasn't at ease, knowing something terrible could happen to someone she loved with no warning. It was a brutal lesson she had learned from her father.

Sam escorted her inside. Lizzie had a fresh pie cooling on the counter and dinner was set in serving dishes on the table. How did she do it? Annabel didn't own serving dishes, period, much less matching ones.

Annabel pointed to the pie. "If your pie goes missing, I can help you find it. I have some experience with that." The words left her mouth tinged with anger. She hadn't meant to say anything about the crappy assignments she had been given at work. It was not professional to speak about her job in her free time or to make passive-aggressive comments. That wasn't the way to deal with Sam. She knew better.

"We all have to start somewhere," Sam said, looking uncomfortable. He glanced at his fiancée, Zoe, and then at Annabel.

Zoe, a librarian, cleared her throat, adjusted her glasses and narrowed her eyes at Sam. It confirmed what Annabel suspected. The entire family knew she was given the worst, most boring assignments in the GGPD.

That made it sting worse and feel as if they were in cahoots against her, even though Ethan, Lizzie, Chris and Zoe had nothing to do with her work duties.

Annabel's tactics to get better assignments were to act with professionalism and grace regardless of the circumstances. She had to rise above, as she had done all her life. Rise above her father's terrible legacy. Rise above her foster parents' crushingly low expectations of her. Rise above the police department's belief she couldn't handle the tough assignments. "Did you handle a lot of cases that involved missing cats and handing out tickets along Main Street?" she asked sweetly.

Chris came in from the porch. "Annabel, I thought I heard your voice." He hugged his sister and then looked at her. "What did I miss?"

"Nothing of note," she said. Before she could tell him anything about what a rotten day it had been, Lizzie broke in.

"It's just us tonight. Ridge and Darcy couldn't

make it. Darcy's on shift at the hospital, and Ridge is working," Lizzie said.

Ridge, Annabel's younger brother, worked in search and rescue, and his high school love, Darcy, was an emergency room doctor at Blackthorn County Hospital. Though they'd parted ways after high school, they'd recently reunited, and Annabel had never seen Ridge so happy.

"I thought Trevor was coming by," Sam said.

"Something came up at work, apparently," Lizzie said.

"Another dead body," Chris said, more a question than a statement.

Lizzie shivered. "He didn't say. He spoke to Ethan when he called. Ethan would be here, but he had a couple of heifers birthing tonight and he's with them in the barn."

Trevor and his FBI team were working with the Granite Gulch Police Department, but the FBI was keeping some details of the Alphabet Killer cases to themselves. The FBI had access to the data in the Alphabet Killer case: the complete autopsies, the ballistics reports and detailed crime scene data, analyzed at their state-of-the-art labs.

Annabel wondered how much Trevor shared with Sam. Some details of the case had been made public knowledge, some had been distributed to the members of the GGPD assigned to the case and some were a matter of speculation.

They sat at the table, and after exchanging pleasantries, the conversation turned to Matthew Colton.

Since Matthew had first made a deal with Sam to reveal the location of their mother's body, he had been the focus of discussions often.

Though speaking of him wasn't the most pleasant topic, Matthew Colton was dying, and he'd engaged them in a game of clues, offering each of his children one word to figure out where their mother had been buried. They were permitted to visit, one Colton per month, on the last Sunday of the month, to receive their clue.

Matthew Colton was serving six consecutive life sentences, and knowing his life would end in prison, perhaps he felt doing something for his children would earn his soul some peace. Matthew did nothing selflessly.

Annabel had considered Matthew was screwing with them, baiting them into visiting him in prison and pretending he was willing to tell them where their mother was buried. Her brothers believed Matthew was genuine in this instance, perhaps attempting one final act to make some amends to his children for what he had done to their family. Nothing would grant him absolution, but at least knowing their mother's final resting place would provide them closure. They could give Saralee a proper burial and service, which Annabel thought her mother would have liked.

Annabel anticipated Matthew Colton was ultimately trying to manipulate them. No way did visits from his children mean anything to him. If he cared about his children, he wouldn't have killed their mother and destroyed their family.

"*Texas*, *hill* and *B*," Zoe said. As a librarian, she had been conducting research on the Colton family and those words, trying to establish connections that the siblings, being too close to the case, hadn't made on their own.

"Annabel, you're planning to visit Matthew, aren't you?" Sam asked.

Why was he on her case? She would go, of course. She hadn't seen her father in over twenty years, and looking at his murderous face, the face that had haunted her dreams for years, was the last thing she wanted to do. But her siblings needed answers, and even though Annabel had her doubts about Matthew telling the truth, she wasn't selfish enough to put her hatred of her father above her brothers. "I will go see him. I've been combing the letters, and he might give something away during our conversation. Hopefully, I can make a connection to what Regina wrote in her letters," Annabel said. "I'd like to spare Chris and Trevor the punishment of seeing him."

Chris patted her hand encouragingly, and Lizzie and Zoe smiled sympathetically. Sam just stared at her.

"Do you want one of us to go with you? I could wait in the car," Sam said.

He was being supportive, but she couldn't help feel he was questioning her strength. "I can do it."

"Alone?"

"I don't know if he'd be willing to speak to me if I brought someone else," Annabel said. "The arrangement you made with him was pretty specific, and I'm sure he'd love for one of us to make a mistake so he can renege on the deal partway through."

As they discussed techniques of dragging more information from their father, Annabel's thoughts switched to Regina Willard and then to Jesse Willard.

Jesse had to have some connection to his sister, Matthew Colton's most loyal fan. Having read the letters Regina had sent Matthew, Annabel had no doubt Regina was unhinged. But Jesse had seemed normal. Could Annabel have been wrong about that? Was Jesse just better at hiding his crazy? Annabel's police instincts were usually reliable. She had dealt with enough nutcases and criminals to intuit when someone was off their rocker.

"Earth to Annabel," Zoe said softly.

"What?" Annabel asked, straightening. "Sorry, I was thinking about the case."

"I asked if you've been seeing anyone," Sam said.

Annabel hated that question, because the answer everyone wanted was she was in a stable relationship. She dated, but it never turned into anything serious. "I've been busy with work and the letters from Matthew," Annabel said. Sam, Ethan and Ridge had found love, and she hoped Chris was next, but a great romance wasn't in the cards for her. She didn't have time. Past relationships ended because she couldn't make a connection with someone. Boyfriends were wary of her, suspecting something dark and twisted slept inside her, because she was the daughter of Granite Gulch's most infamous serial killer.

Chris had found love once, but it had ended tragically. He had lost his wife, and he hadn't been able to move on yet. The house he had built for Laura remained empty. He couldn't move into it and, instead, lived in an apartment over Double G Cakes and Pies. They made the best desserts in town, and Chris was lucky he wasn't a hundred pounds overweight. His PI job kept him hopping. Every time Annabel visited her brother, she couldn't resist stopping into the Double G for a dessert and to visit with her good friend Mia.

Even so, thinking about the woman Chris had lost made Annabel sad. Chris could have been happy with a family of his own, but instead he worked too much and kept any prospects at bay.

"You need some balance in your life," Sam said.

Annabel felt her defensiveness rise. No one criticized Chris or Trevor about their lack of love lives. "Just because you fell in love doesn't mean everyone else will."

Sam smiled at Zoe, and if Annabel didn't love them both so much, she would have gagged at the sugary sweetness in that shared look.

"We just want you to be happy," Lizzie said. "And lately, it seems like you go to work and then go home and read those letters." She shuddered. "You deserve more. You deserve happiness."

She was happy. She was finally a police officer, a dream she had chased without her family's approval. Achieving that goal meant a lot to her. Proving herself meant she could ask for better assignments. "Until we get this resolved with Matthew, I'm satisfied with my life and plenty busy."

The conversation moved on, and Annabel was glad the focus had shifted away from her.

After dinner, Annabel joined Chris on the back porch. She sat next to him on the patio sofa, and they propped their feet on the wooden coffee table.

"You know he goes after you because he worries," Chris said. "We all do."

He was referring to Sam. Annabel understood. Her younger brother might be one of Granite Gulch's best detectives, but he had a lot to learn about his place in the family. He didn't get to call the shots in her life. "I worry about you all, too. Your PI work puts you in tough spots. Ridge is running around in dangerous terrain, and Sam is working the streets, searching for criminals, and Trevor…well, who knows what he's up to, but I guarantee it involves dangerous people."

"I know. I worry about everyone, too. With you, it's different. We lost Josie," Chris said.

His words hit her in the gut. Annabel wanted more than anything to find her sister, work out whatever problems were keeping them apart and for Josie to be part of their lives. "I know." It was painful for them to have Josie far out of reach.

"And Mom," Chris said. "And Laura. It's the Colton curse. Bad things happen to Colton women."

Annabel had thought about that before. "I think about Mom and Josie, too."

"I know you do," Chris said. "I want you all to find the happiness I had with Laura, even though I feel cheated out of time with her. When I see Sam, Ethan and Ridge, I envy their happiness, and I worry about Zoe, Lizzie and Darcy."

Annabel squeezed her twin's hand. "Nothing bad will happen. Matthew is behind bars, and he can't hurt us anymore. We're staying close and watching out for each other." Though Sam, Ethan and Ridge had been through difficult struggles in recent months, they had been strong and had protected the women they loved.

Chris shrugged. "Except Matthew found a groupie who seems to believe he is brilliant and worth following in his footsteps."

It was disturbing to Annabel, as well. "I wish the media would stop dragging out Matthew Colton stories and parading them around with parallels to Regina. That only encourages her, and whoever else may have the unbalanced idea to commit crimes to become famous."

"Matthew seems amused by Regina's antics."

"Matthew having any source of happiness burns me," Annabel said. "That's part of the reason I don't want to visit him. He loves jerking us around. He couldn't get us to visit any other way, so he dangles the one thing that compels us."

"You still think it's a game with no ending?" Chris asked.

"Why not ask us to visit and tell us where Mom is buried without clues and cryptic messages spread across many months?" Annabel asked. "He's dying. It has to have dawned on him that he could die before we receive our clues. Then, where are we? He can enjoy watching us twist and squirm and beg him for information. In any case, who knows if these clues even mean anything? One word is hardly enough. If it were that easy to find Mom, we would have found her. Or the authorities would have found her twenty years ago."

"No way to know unless we follow through on our visits," Chris said.

"After I go, it's your turn."

Chris sighed. "Don't remind me. I'm not looking forward to talking to that man any more than you are, but I'll do it. I want Mom to have a real burial."

"We'll get through this," Annabel said, resting her head on her brother's shoulder. "Coltons can withstand anything, especially when we stand together."

"Even for a small town, you and I seem to land the most boring assignments in America," Luis said, sliding his gun into its holster at his hip and closing his locker.

Annabel agreed with him, but she had been trying not to focus on it. Talking about it fed into her anger and frustration.

"It wasn't like this before I was your partner. I actually apprehended criminals in the process of committing crimes. I responded to home invasions."

Guilt hit her, and she tried not to turn that guilt into more anger at Sam. He had something to do with her crappy assignments, and it scorched her. Shouldn't he want to help her in her career, not hold her back?

"Then again, my wife is happier with you as my

partner. She doesn't need to worry as much. I'm not in danger tracking a culprit who trampled a flower garden. Especially when that culprit turns out to be two-year-old twins who were chasing their ball into a grouchy neighbor's yard."

Annabel pictured Zoe looking at Sam, and her anger flamed hotter. Her and Luis's dull assignments were intentional and unfair. Other rookies weren't assigned only boring tasks. Sure, she should pay her dues, and she understood it was more than her rookie status keeping her away from the most interesting and dangerous case in the GGPD, the Alphabet Killer murders. She was tangentially related to the case because of her connection, no matter how severed, to Matthew Colton, and Chief Murray wouldn't involve her directly because he was worried about a slick-talking defense lawyer twisting the facts of the case and pointing to prejudicial handling and analysis of evidence by a Colton.

But another day of missing pies and cats, and Annabel would lose it.

"Give me a minute. I need to talk to the chief before we head out," Annabel said.

"I'll grab some coffees," Luis said.

Annabel strode to Chief Murray's office. She reached for the door handle and took a deep breath. Getting this off her chest would save her sanity. Even if Chief Murray told her to suck it up and deal with it, at least he'd be aware she knew she was being treated unfairly. It wasn't just about her. Luis was bored to tears, too.

Annabel almost lost her nerve when she saw Sam speaking with him. Sam was seated across from Chief Murray's desk, slightly reclined in the chair, looking relaxed and buddy-buddy with the chief. Maybe it was better Sam was in the room. Both needed to hear what she had to say, and this would save her from repeating herself. Sam might be dismissive with her, but Chief Murray was a fair man and would hear her out.

She knocked once on the door and then opened it, stepping inside and closing the door behind her. She'd had enough conflicts in her life to know rushing in with guns blazing, firing accusations around the room, wasn't the best technique with men who liked to be right.

The chief prided himself on making levelheaded and fair decisions. Sam believed he was above reproach.

"'Morning, Annabel. What can I do for you?" Chief Murray asked.

Annabel glanced at Sam. He didn't seem annoyed, only curious. To this point, Annabel had kept her head down and worked. She didn't complain to her bosses, and she didn't bad-mouth her work assignments to anyone on the force. Her dear friend Mia had heard an earful about her terrible assignments, but that was what great friends were for.

"Yesterday, I handed out five parking tickets, looked for a missing cat, which turned out to be sleeping in the owner's upstairs windowsill, and took a report for a missing blueberry pie. My prime suspects in that case are the baker's children, whose faces were smeared with cinnamon and blue jam, but who swore they had nothing to do with the pie's disappearance." She took a deep breath. "I graduated at the top of my class from the police academy. I'm not above the simple assignments, but why am I assigned all the dull assignments in the department?"

Chief Murray looked at her and said nothing for a long moment. "Anything else?"

"My partner is an experienced police officer. He has a lot to teach me and can offer much more to the town, but not when he's shackled to me, the magnet for boring."

She had made her point, and she waited for Chief Murray to respond.

Sam looked part worried and part admiring.

Chief Murray leaned back in his chair, folding his hands across his stomach. "You've excelled at the tasks you've been assigned."

How hard was writing parking tickets and taking reports? "Yes, sir."

"I've noted the contributions you've made to other cases. The Alphabet Killer case in particular."

She was surprised he had remembered she had worked with the letters on that case. "Yes, sir."

He leaned forward. "Luis is on vacation the next two days, and I had planned for you to work the information phone—"

Annabel could have fallen asleep at the idea of sitting at the information desk for two full shifts. When Luis had mentioned he was taking a couple of days off to celebrate his wedding anniversary with his wife, Annabel had hoped she would be given a temporary partner. The information phone was the worst fate in work tasks.

"But I have an assignment for you, something you might find more enjoyable."

Her interest piqued.

"A stakeout at Willard's Farm, the farm owned and operated by Jesse Willard, Regina Willard's half brother."

At the mention of Jesse's name, heat spiraled through her. An exciting assignment for sure, putting her closer to the Alphabet Killer case.

"We don't have evidence connecting Jesse to the crimes, but he could be aiding his sister in some way, providing her shelter or lying for her. We've spoken to him several times, and he's been questioned by the FBI. Since we don't have anything on him, we can't lean on him. Watch his place for signs of Regina, or anything that connects him to the Alphabet Killer murders. You have an eye for detail, you're hungry and you might notice something others have missed."

Annabel was thrilled with both the assignment and the chief's recognition of her abilities.

"Chief—" Sam protested, but the chief held up his hand, silencing him.

The chief didn't like to be argued with, and given that much of his control had been taken by the FBI leading the investigation, he wanted absolute control over other decisions in his precinct.

"Familiarize yourself with Regina Willard's file. She is likely in disguise. Take the department's high-powered camera and snap pictures of anything that looks suspicious. Even if it turns out to be nothing, it's worth the chance. Stay in your undercover vehicle and call for backup if you see anyone who looks like Regina."

"Yes, sir," Annabel said, thrilled to have a real assignment for the first time since joining the GGPD.

"If you see Regina, do not approach her," Chief Murray said. "The FBI is developing a profile of Regina, but they don't know what sets her off. Your age and hair color make you a match for her victims."

"My name doesn't start with *G*," Annabel said.

"I doubt taking one more life, even if it's not in keeping with her alphabetical system, would give her pause."

"Thank you, Chief Murray. I'll do my best."

"I know you will. Don't let me down."

Annabel practically skipped from the chief's office and resisted the immature urge to stick out her tongue at her brother. Her hard work had finally paid off.

She hadn't made it to Luis to share the great news when Sam caught up with her. "Annabel, do you want me to come with you on the stakeout?"

Annabel shook her head. "I've got this."

"Promise me you won't try to prove something out there. You heard the chief. First sign of trouble and you call for help," Sam said.

"I understood what he said. I'll be careful. You don't have anything to worry about," Annabel said. She kissed her brother's cheek, reminding herself it was good he was protective of her, and rushed off to meet Luis. She could face their inevitably tedious day knowing something new was waiting for her tomorrow.

If she did a good job with the stakeout, she was on her way to shedding her rookie status and having a real career as a police officer in Granite Gulch.

Jesse had a list of worries a mile long. Low on supplies, too much to do, the irrigation system was broken in one of his cotton fields and he could not stop thinking about two brunettes in his life making him crazy: Regina, whom he could not find. No one knew where she was or even her last address. She had lost touch with mutual friends and their few remaining family members. And the other brunette was distracting in an entirely different way. The police officer from the station had been on his mind.

He had felt sure he would lose it on the Colton brothers who were bent on pinning the recent rash of killings on Regina. They wouldn't listen to reason, and they didn't believe him when he said he didn't know where Regina was.

Driving his pickup into Granite Gulch, Jesse stopped at the Green and Grow. It was his favorite shop in town, catering to both commercial and residential clients. They had greenhouses filled with plants, piles of compost, manure and soil for the home gardener and an impressive array of supplies for fixing farm problems. When he needed a bigger shipment, he ordered from a supplier in Fort Worth, but the Green and Grow had pulled him out of a tight spot many times.

Jesse ignored the suspicious and curious looks he received from the residents in town. People were talking trash about him and Regina. He didn't know how to combat the rumors except by going about his business, working hard and hoping the interest in his sister fizzled after the real murderer was found. Growing up, he had become accustomed to ignoring the rude stares and hurtful words of others. His father had been a real piece of work, and Jesse had gone to school hungry, dirty and tired on more than one occasion. Those experiences had calloused him to gossips.

He entered the garden store, lifting his hand in greeting to Bernie, the sales clerk. She didn't gossip, and he appreciated it. Her life and interests were in gardening. She could talk for hours about her plants and the growing habits of certain vegetation, but she was mum when it came to talking about other people. She might be the only one in Granite Gulch who didn't.

After he placed his order, he paid and walked around to the back of the store to load his truck. He usually had one of his farmhands with him, but with Grace on an alternative assignment, and since he hadn't found anyone to replace the no-show who'd disappeared, he couldn't spare anyone else. They were coming into the busy season. His crops needed to be watered and fertilized on schedule, the soil tested, animals fed and cared for, and the fences mended. He'd run a produce stand on the side of the road the past several years, and it had generated some income. Usually, he had one of his farmhands at the stand to talk about the produce and collect money, but to save on staffing expenses, he would set out a tin can and hope the people of Granite Gulch were honest enough to pay him.

After he loaded his vehicle, he considered stopping at the diner for lunch but figured he couldn't spare the time. Turning onto Main Street, he'd hit the highway in a few miles and beat feet back to his farm.

He slowed when he recognized the policewoman from the other day walking along Main Street with another officer.

The impulse to stop and talk to her was strong. Parking along Main Street was busy this time of day, but he could find a spot. What would he say to her? Would he look desperate and aggressive? Their exchange had been more unspoken than verbal, but perhaps she had felt nothing. Did she know he was Regina Willard's brother? Given the smallness of the Granite Gulch Police Department and the high-profile nature of the Alphabet Killer murders, Jesse guessed everyone on the police force was involved, if only marginally. The FBI had been brought in to investigate, but since the Alphabet Killer had not been apprehended, they needed to catch a break.

The female officer smiled at something her older, male partner said, and she looked even more beautiful. She had her hair tied in a ponytail, and it swung as she strutted down the sidewalk. She and her partner walked into the diner.

Jesse changed his mind about having enough time. He would make time. A second chance to talk to the pretty officer was slim, considering he rarely drove to town, and he doubted she would visit the farm.

Jesse parked and started toward the diner. He was hungry, and it had been a while since he'd eaten. The diner made the best tuna melt and apple pie. His stomach growled just thinking about it.

"Willard!"

At the sound of his name, he turned. Tug Johnson, who had worked for him on and off over the years, was jogging toward him. The last he'd heard, Tug had left town. What had brought him back to Granite Gulch?

"Hey, how are you?" Jesse asked. He stayed on friendly terms with his employees and former employees. With the exception of a few bad seeds, he had been successful. The farming community in Texas was close-knit, and it didn't help him to make enemies.

"Doing okay. I was out in California for a while, but the work dried up. I even had a temp job in an office. Came back this way for the growing season."

"Looking for honest work?" Jesse asked. He didn't lie to his employees about the amount of work or how labor intensive it was. Working for him meant a decent wage, but in return, he expected a fair day's toil.

"Mind if I come by the farm later? I have a girl now. She's counting on me," Tug said.

"Sounds good," Jesse said, relieved he might have

found someone to replace the farmhand who'd quit without notice.

Tug shifted on his feet and adjusted his blue ball cap. "I heard about that mess with your sister. What are you going to do?"

Jesse hated confronting rumors, and he didn't know what Tug wanted him to say, except maybe divulge some tidbit of information about Regina that would garner Tug some attention at happy hour as he shared the latest gossip. But an overreaction on his part would be telling, and Jesse didn't want to encourage the rumors by feeding them a temper tantrum. "The police are looking for Regina. They have questions for her. If I see her, I'll send her their way." Sticking to the facts would keep him out of trouble.

Tug touched the brim of his hat. "You're not worried she'll come looking for you?"

"Unlikely. I haven't spoken to her in years, and she's been good about ignoring me when she doesn't want to talk." Regina had been that way since they were children. She sulked, she brooded and when she was ready to discuss her problems, she'd find Jesse.

"I hear she has an ax to grind with everyone. An ax or whatever weapon she can find," Tug said.

Jesse hid his annoyance. The implication Regina was the Alphabet Killer was off base. "Regina can be difficult, but she's not dangerous."

Tug pulled on the waistband of his pants, hitching them higher. "I don't know about that. Careful about turning a blind eye to a problem. You live way out there alone. Can't know what could happen in the middle of the night."

Jesse enjoyed the solitude and privacy of his farm, located just inside the borders of Granite Gulch but far enough away from the busiest part of town. Jesse could have hired staff to live on the premises, but his farm wasn't big enough to require it, and he enjoyed having the farm to himself sometimes. He had a carriage house he had been renovating, but that pet project wasn't leading anywhere fast, given his time and money restrictions. "I'll be okay, but I appreciate your concern."

He tipped his hat to Tug. "If you'll excuse me, I need to see about wrangling some lunch."

Tug said goodbye, and Jesse continued on to the diner. He guessed Tug wouldn't show up at the farm later. That conversation felt like Tug digging for information about Regina. If Jesse didn't find help soon, he'd start actively looking for someone, which took even more time.

Entering the diner and removing his hat, Jesse scanned for the police officer. She should be easy to spot; both her uniform and her beauty would stand out head and shoulders above others. The diner was crowded. Waitresses and waiters in their navy pants and crisp white shirts, their green aprons tied around their waists, moved through the diner with trays of food and drinks. Jesse stopped and slid to the side to allow two older women with walkers move toward the register.

Maybe this was crazy and he should grab his lunch

to go. He was nervous, which didn't happen often. But he had come this far, and it was just a conversation. If she did not want to talk to him, he could take a hint and back away.

He looked around and didn't see her. Just as he was about to give up searching, he spotted her brunette ponytail at the end of the counter.

She was next to the other officer, drinking a soda and eating a club sandwich. Despite the busy lunch hour, Jesse was pleased the stool next to hers was open. Maybe his luck was finally changing. Moving through the crowd, he pretended not to hear his and Regina's names whispered. He hadn't done anything wrong, and he wouldn't slink around town with shame hanging on his shoulders.

"Mind if I sit here?" he asked as he tapped the seat next to her.

She turned toward him, smiling. The sense of connection and rightness arced between them.

Though her smile faded and her eyes turned wary, she gestured to the seat. If she hadn't known who he was on their first meeting, she knew now. "Please, help yourself. Seat's open." Her voice was warm and inviting.

He sat. He wanted to see her name tag, but from the position she was sitting, he couldn't read it. His interest in her was unusual for him. Though he'd had some girlfriends, he hadn't worked at a relationship, hadn't pursued women who didn't come to him easily. He hadn't mastered the art of flirting. Relationships fell into place, at least for a while. He didn't think his relationship with the police officer would be anything like that. If he wanted her attention, he'd need to work for it. That intrigued him.

The Alphabet Killer investigation wasn't one he was interested in discussing. Did they have anything else in common? Why was he tongue-tied when he was near this woman? Even at the police precinct when he had run into her, he felt like an oaf who couldn't construct a coherent sentence. "Are you new to Granite Gulch?" Jesse asked. He'd purchased his farm ten years ago. Though he hadn't become friendly with many people outside his farmhands and business associates, he'd have remembered seeing someone like her around. She was a head turner and hard to forget.

She inclined her head, and her ponytail swung to the side. "Not new to Granite Gulch. New to the police force," she said. Hitting the word *police* hard made her point, if her uniform hadn't already.

"I work on a farm nearby. I make it to town now and then," he said.

If she showed a spark of interest, now and then could become often and eagerly.

She didn't say anything and looked instead at her sandwich. Jesse couldn't let the conversation go that easily. He wanted to feel the way he did at the police precinct when they had been chest to chest, thigh to thigh. That moment had been like a drug in his veins, and he craved the high again.

Despite the crowd, he felt the snap of their connection as if they were the only two people in the diner. How could she not feel the attraction, too? He glanced down at his clothes. Dirty and dusty, indicating he worked with his hands. Maybe that was a turnoff to her. Not a lot of women fantasized about dating a farmer. Or if they did harbor any fantasies, they died quickly when they realized it was tough work and long hours. Jesse wouldn't have traded it for anything. Working the land brought him a great sense of pride. "What did you do before becoming a police officer?"

"I was a park ranger," she said.

She wasn't disgusted by being outdoors, and he liked that. For him, the sun and the wind were essential. City living, with its tall buildings blocking the sun and creating a wind tunnel out of a gentle breeze, suffocated him.

Her partner shot him an appraising look. Did that look have anything to do with Regina or just that he was another man talking to a beautiful woman?

The radio clipped to her shoulder beeped. She answered it immediately and brought it close to her ear. The message crackled, and then both the woman and her partner stood. "Officers responding."

"See you around," she said as she and her partner tossed money on the counter and hurried from the diner.

It wasn't the conversation he'd hoped for with the striking brunette, but it was a start.

Annabel didn't know if dispatch had been given the go-ahead for her and Luis to receive actual police assignments, but they were en route to break up a street fight. Most street clashes in Granite Gulch were Friday-night bar brawls. A daytime fight? Annabel didn't know what she and Luis would find, but she was ready. Her adrenaline was pumping hard and not just from the report of a fight.

Jesse Willard had turned her head around. She should want nothing to do with him, and she should have been borderline cold to him. Once he had started talking to her, it was impossible to ignore him.

She and Luis ran the two blocks along Main Street and turned into an alley next to the Bar and Saloon. Four men total, three wailing on the other. The victim was slumped on the ground. The alley dumpster was overflowing with the stink of skunked beer and rotting chicken. Annabel's stomach soured, but she focused.

"Police! Show me your hands!" Annabel said, drawing her gun.

"Your hands! Now!" Luis echoed.

At their command, two of the men took off in the opposite direction. The third assailant put his hands on his head. The victim was not moving, and Annabel called on her radio. "I need an ambulance on Main Street, next to the Bar and Saloon."

"Go, Annabel. I have these two," Luis said.

Heeding her partner's experience, she chased after the men who had fled the scene. When she reached the end of the alley, she looked left and right. They were gone. A car engine revved, and a light blue pickup truck pulled out of the alley a block away.

The truck had a large rusted spot along the passenger side. It turned away from her, skidding on the dusty road. She was too far away to read the license plate, but she could provide a basic description of the pickup and a rough sketch of the suspects.

She clicked her radio. "I have a blue pickup fleeing the scene of a crime. Older model. Two suspects. Consider them dangerous and proceed with caution." She jogged back to assist Luis.

Luis had one man cuffed and seated against the exterior wall of the saloon. Luis was leaning over the victim, checking his neck for a pulse. As their backup and the sound of an ambulance siren approached, a crowd began to form.

"Sir, stay with us. Help is on the way," Annabel said. She spoke to the man, watching the rise and fall of his chest and hoping he survived. He had cuts on his face and from what she had witnessed, likely other injuries to the rest of his body.

Annabel felt someone watching her. She lifted her head and saw Jesse Willard. He stepped toward her with a first-aid kit in his hand.

He knelt on the ground and opened the kit. He took a fresh gauze pad and pressed it over a cut on the man's face.

Jesse seemed to know what he was doing.

"How can I help?" she asked.

Jesse glanced at her. "Not sure there's anything we can do until the ambulance gets here. I have some medical training, but he needs a doctor."

The ambulance arrived, and the crowd parted to

allow the paramedics through. Annabel's priorities became securing the victim into the care of the EMTs and paramedics. They would take him to Blackthorn County Hospital. Detectives would be sent to the hospital to question him when he was able to talk.

Luis led the remaining attacker to their squad car. He'd be questioned for information on his associates. Something about the wildness of his eyes and the way he walked made Annabel think this was drug related. A drug deal gone bad or a territory dispute? Granite Gulch was a small town and not without its problems.

Annabel turned to thank Jesse, but he was gone.

Chapter 3

Annabel had pulled out her books from the police academy and had reviewed her notes on conducting a stakeout the night before. Though the chance of spotting Regina Willard walking around Willard's Farm was low, she wanted to be prepared. This was her first assignment without Luis outside routine police work, and Chief Murray was watching her closely. She wouldn't make a foolish mistake and have the chief believing he had made an error in giving her this task. She had stuck her neck out, claimed she was ready for more and she would rise to the challenge.

Feeling guilty for watching Willard's Farm when Jesse had been helpful at the scene of the beating outside the Bar and Saloon, Annabel reminded herself a stakeout wasn't personal. This was about stopping a killer and following every lead, regardless of how remote the chances of finding Regina were. Annabel didn't owe Jesse anything, and even though he had seemed nice, plenty of things in Annabel's life had seemed good until they weren't. She had happily lived in the big farmhouse with her parents and siblings, her home with Mama Jean had been wonderful, but those things had been snatched away. Jesse might seem nice, but he could be a sociopath. Being attracted to him was utterly confusing, and she did not make good decisions in her personal life. This stakeout wasn't personal, no matter her feelings for Jesse Willard. Having a crush on someone involved with a case didn't supersede her responsibilities to remain professional and objective.

Annabel drove to Willard's Farm and parked across from the main farmhouse on a public road. With acres of land, crops, the barns and outbuildings, it was difficult to find a good angle to see everything.

Staying on the main road, Annabel would note who came and went from the farm. She would check license plates and look for anyone off schedule. If Regina was hiding at her brother's farm, she had to show herself at some point. She'd need to go out, if for no other reason than to search for victims or to mail more sicko letters to Matthew Colton.

Annabel had checked the aerial view of the farm on a map and didn't see other access roads, but the data she'd been using was at least three months old. She would circle the property later and see if Jesse had another way onto his property Regina could use to move about discreetly.

Annabel made herself comfortable and tried not to think about someone creeping up behind her. Her undercover police vehicle had extra mirrors to give her a 360-degree view around the car, but she couldn't look everywhere at once. Chief Murray had sent her out alone. He must believe the chances of someone approaching her were slim. She agreed with that assessment, but being farther from town in a location she wasn't familiar with made her uneasy.

She settled into her seat and focused. It was ten minutes before two in the afternoon. According to the police department's file on Jesse Willard, his farmhands changed shifts at two. As cars drove up the road and turned into the driveway, Annabel scrawled notes. A few minutes later, other cars left the ranch.

Regina could be hiding in one of the cars, and Annabel was tempted to stop the vehicles and search them, but Chief Murray had been clear. She was only to watch. If she had suspicions about more going on and that someone, Jesse or a farmhand, was hiding Regina, she would report it and return with a proper search warrant. Or rather, another officer would. Since Annabel's last name was Colton, any evidence she found would be subject to question by a decent defense attorney. A lawyer could claim she was emotionally invested in the case and lacking impartiality. Though Annabel knew the difference and wouldn't make a legal mistake that could cause Regina to go free, it was better to do as Chief Murray asked.

They would find Regina and not make mistakes along the way. The case would be strong, and Regina would spend the rest of her life in prison. At least she would as soon as they located her.

Willard's Farm was well maintained. Annabel recalled the farm ten years ago when it had been a non-productive, run-down eyesore. The former owner had lived on the farm his whole life, and after he passed, he had no family to leave it to and the land was sold.

Jesse obviously took pride in his farm and his home. The farmhouse looked as if it had a new roof and a fresh coat of paint on the exterior, the shutters shining in the afternoon sun. The porch had a few chairs, and the gardens around the house were tidy and blooming with pink and purple flowers.

Behind the house, extending as far as she could see, the rows of crops were lush and green. The barn was painted red, and farmhands were moving around the property with purpose.

Could Jesse Willard be hiding his sister? Family was important. The Coltons had been separated when they were children. Annabel hadn't stopped longing for and looking for her brothers. They had been sent to different foster homes across Blackthorn County, and it had been difficult to keep in touch.

Annabel had reconnected with Chris in high school. Despite the initial distance and awkwardness between them, she and Chris had gotten along well. He had even assisted her with a bully in high school who had been pestering her and whose harassment had turned physical.

She and Chris had located the rest of their family after high school. Only Josie was still missing.

Josie had wanted nothing to do with them. Annabel had thought she would outgrow it. The family had been through a lot, and as children and then teenagers, they'd each had their personal struggles in coping with their father's crimes and the death of their mother and dissolution of their family. Their experiences in foster care had run the gamut, and life had been hard for each of them in different ways. Only Josie hadn't come around.

If Josie came knocking on her door needing help, Annabel would assist her without questions. Is that how Jesse felt about his sister?

Annabel's attention caught on a woman walking across the property. She had her hair pulled up into her hat, but she was the right build for Regina. Annabel used her binoculars to get a better look at the woman's face. The woman stopped in front of the house, and Jesse Willard came down the steps. They didn't touch, but a warm familiarity existed between them. Was she his girlfriend? If she was, why did that make Annabel both jealous and disappointed? She and Jesse weren't dating. Annabel brushed aside the ridiculous notion and ignored the flip-flop of her belly thinking about Jesse taking her out.

Then the woman removed her hat, and locks of brown, curly hair fell down to her shoulders. When she angled her face, Annabel could see this was not Regina Willard. The woman was too young. Regina could be in disguise, but no disguise was that good.

Annabel's heart caught in her throat when Jesse looked in her direction. He did a double take, and his shoulders fell. Would he talk to her? Ignore her? Should she approach him? Though she had been clear on her assignment, seeing him made that clarity disappear. All she wanted was to talk to Jesse Willard.

"I have a call into the vet about Misty," Grace said. "Her hair has lost its luster, and she's been acting strange."

Jesse had noticed his mare's change in behavior, too. She was lethargic and tired too often. He'd tried changing her diet, but it hadn't helped. "Thanks. Let me know what the doc has to say." When he knew what was wrong and could fix it, he would stop worrying.

Jesse had given Grace alternative assignments, but she still looked tired. She hadn't complained, but he had another idea. "I'm planning to hire someone to help me around the house. It's getting to be too much. I've been working on the remodel of the carriage house, and it's taking a lot of my time. You want to try switching up your duties?" Working in the house would keep her out of the hot sun and away from backbreaking work. If she put up her feet on the couch from time to time, he was good with that.

Grace inclined her head. "Do you feel obligated to offer because I'm pregnant?" She set her hand over her stomach protectively.

Not obligated. But he was a good boss, and he valued her as an employee. "I've been thinking about it for a while, and you've risen to every challenge."

"Are you saying working in the house would be a challenge?" Grace asked.

"Being closer to me and putting up with my grumpiness? I would say that, yes, that would be a challenge for anyone," Jesse said.

Grace threw her arms around his neck. "You're a good man, Jesse. I would be happy to help you with running your house. Thanks."

Jesse hugged her but not too tight. "I'll have a list of tasks for you tomorrow. Why don't you head off and pick up Noah from school?"

Grace had arrived at work late and had stayed longer to make up the time. Not at his insistence, but that was who Grace was. Jesse didn't want to lose her.

"I'll do that. See you tomorrow."

As Grace walked toward her car, Jesse looked back at the car parked near the end of his driveway on the public access road. He couldn't see the driver with the glare of the sun against the window. He didn't get many visitors to the farm. The last uninvited visitors had been the FBI, who had questioned him at length about his sister.

Were they back? Or was it a media outlet poking around about Regina? He'd hoped it was a lost tourist who would check their GPS and move on, but clearly that wasn't the case. It had been a solid five minutes, and the car remained rooted in place.

Jesse didn't want to be harassed. He didn't want his employees hassled. Any altercation made the situation worse. He was the owner of the farm, and while diplomacy wasn't on his mind, he forced himself to appear calm. When he was younger, he'd been a hothead, and that behavior only led to trouble. Deciding to play nice, he went inside the house, brewed a cup of coffee and carried it down the driveway.

The mug had his farm's name on it, Willard's Farm, and whoever was in the car could drink the coffee and keep the mug as long as they left him alone.

He glanced both ways before crossing the street. When he was closer, he had his first view of the driver. He almost spilled the coffee down his jeans. The police officer from the precinct he'd seen again at the All Night Diner was seated in the car, watching him. He had been thinking about those blue eyes for days.

What were the chances this was a social visit? He guessed next to nil.

He motioned for her to roll down her window. Keeping his relationship with the police and FBI friendly had been his intent, and now that he saw who was watching him, he was glad it wasn't a reporter. This was an opportunity to talk to the pretty policewoman. Perhaps he could charm her into seeing his side of the situation.

"Good afternoon. I thought I would properly introduce myself. I'm Jesse Willard."

"I know who you are, Mr. Willard. This is your farm. I'm Annabel Colton."

Her last name was familiar, too. Same name as the detective in the GGPD and the FBI agent who had grilled him for hours about Regina and who were related to Matthew Colton, a serial killer serving a life sentence in prison. It seemed in Granite Gulch, investigations were a family affair.

He extended to her the cup of coffee. "Thought you might like this. Push through the afternoon lull."

She reached out and accepted the mug. "Smells good."

So did she. Even with the aroma of coffee in his nostrils, a light floral fragrance wafted from the car, her scent.

"I can't drink much, though. No facilities," she said, nodding at the car.

He leaned on the roof of the car, trying to look cool and figuring he missed it by a mile. She was under his skin, and he wanted to open the car door and pull her into his arms. Slender and strong, a combination he liked. He bet she held her own. "Planning on being here long?"

She nodded.

A stakeout? She was spying on him. "Tell me what you're looking for, and I'll save you a lot of time and trouble." He already knew, but he wanted her to say it plain.

"We're looking for your sister, Regina Willard."

Annoyance plucked at him. "Regina is my half sister, and she isn't here. The police and the FBI have scoured every inch of my farm. I haven't seen her in six years. I've tried contacting her directly and through friends, and I can't reach her."

Annabel frowned. "She might turn up."

"Unlikely. Regina and I aren't close."

Annabel took a sip of the coffee. "Thanks for the drink."

She sounded as if she was ending the conversation, and he wasn't ready to let this go. He didn't want her outside his farm spying on him, and it bothered him immensely that she was working against him. "I already told your kin if Regina shows up, I will encourage her to speak with you all."

"I know what you told my brothers."

Her brothers had likely told her that he was the brother of a murderer. They were wrong on that count, and it bothered Jesse that her opinion might be shaded by theirs.

Why did the FBI and police want to pin this mess on him and Regina? He had nothing to do with Regina, and he didn't believe she had anything to do with the murders. "I've been cooperative and helpful. I've been a good sport about this. But it's costing me business, and if folks see you sitting outside my farm, that makes me look bad, like I've done something wrong."

He saw compassion flicker across her face. Would she give up on the stakeout and report the truth to her superiors and her brothers? Regina was not on the farm.

"I'm sorry, Mr. Willard. I'm doing my job."

"How can I make you understand? The last time I spoke to my sister, she was a bitter, angry woman. She thinks the world is out to get her, and she's more likely to be hiding in her apartment somewhere binging on wine and television than doing the things you have implied she's done."

Things that made him sick to think about. Killing innocent women based on their names? Only a crazy person would see logic in that, and while Regina was sad, and he suspected clinically depressed, she wasn't homicidal.

"Do you know where this apartment may be?"

He had been speaking generally. He didn't know where Regina was. How many times and how many different ways could he say it? "I want to clear the air more than almost anyone in Granite Gulch. Regina's had a hard life, and she doesn't need this extra stress."

"Hard life how?"

Guilt and protectiveness rose up inside him, creating a volatile cocktail that felt like anger. "Our father was not a nice man."

"Lots of people have parents who are terrible. It doesn't excuse committing a crime."

She spoke as if it was a done deal, and she was sure Regina was guilty. Regina didn't cope with things well. She hid and buried her head in the sand. If she had heard the police wanted to speak with her, that would only make her withdraw further inward.

He wouldn't betray Regina by revealing family secrets, by telling Annabel the types of abuse his mother had rescued them from. Jesse carried a lot of guilt that his mother had left Regina behind. She had said she didn't have a choice, but at the time, Jesse had wanted his big sister to flee with them more than anything.

"Regina found happiness with someone as an adult, and he left her. She didn't handle it well." When Regina had been in a relationship, one that had seemed stable, it was the first time Jesse recalled seeing Regina smile and laugh. He had been worried when the engagement ended. Regina had her wedding gown and had seemed happy to be getting married. She would have had a chance to have a family and do the things she had been denied. A loving, attentive mother and a gentle, yet firm father who ate dinner together and took family vacations to the lake. Granted, Regina hadn't said she wanted those things, but Jesse had imagined her new life being happy.

"What do you mean she didn't handle it well?" Annabel asked.

He didn't intend to give Annabel reasons to believe Regina was unstable. "She grieved for the loss of her fiancé. She was obsessed with winning him back. I told her no man was worth the nonsense she was carrying on about, and she should let go. Anything was better than being emotionally attached to someone who didn't want her in his life. I suggested online dating, therapy, joining a soccer team. But Regina wasn't ready to move on." She had been consumed by her anger, and she didn't want his advice. Not that he was an expert in love. "My dating history isn't pristine. I was the wrong person to advise her."

"You have a history of having problems with women you've dated?"

She was misinterpreting what he was saying. Her question didn't sound related to Regina. It sounded personal. He could be misreading her, but he felt something simmering unsaid between them. "Don't jump to conclusions. I'm not married. Obviously, I don't have the key to making a relationship work either."

Annabel frowned, and her eyes narrowed slightly. She looked beautiful when she was thinking. She had a lot going on between the ears.

"Do you remember anything about your sister that would make you think she could harm someone? Maybe her bitterness turned violent? Maybe her emotions boiled over, and she acted out?"

She was weaving a twisted tale, leaping from one conclusion to another, making it sound as if Regina was crazy and violent and capable of murder. He didn't take kindly to someone talking garbage about his kin, and something in him snapped. "Are you asking me to help you pin those murders on Regina? I won't do that. I have answered these questions again and again for your brothers. I am done being questioned like a criminal. I have done nothing wrong, and I don't appreciate the implication that I would break the law and hide someone or that I'm withholding critical information. I know there's some psycho out there killing women. Do you think I'm indifferent to that?" His mother had been a victim of violence, and violence against women was something he would not stand for. He worried about Grace, with her long brown hair, being a target.

Annabel seemed uncertain what to say. "I'm sure you're not indifferent to it. But we're putting all our resources into finding the Alphabet Killer, and we have strong reasons to believe Regina knows something about the murders."

Jesse tried to put a lid on his anger. "Can you take it or do you just dish it out? You ask me questions about my sister, like I'm supposed to have any rational reasons for why someone would run around Blackthorn County killing women. You're the cop. Tell me about your father. Does what you know about him follow with Matthew Colton, serial killer? From what I understand, he's the mastermind behind the Alphabet Killer murders."

She inhaled sharply. "Matthew Colton has been in contact with Regina Willard. She's obsessed with him, but he is not directing her to kill anyone."

If she believed that, she had blinders on when it came to Matthew Colton. Jesse had read about the case online. The media was having a great time connecting the two cases, drawing on similarities between the murders. "Matthew Colton is making you dance like puppets. Why don't you turn your screws on him? Make him tell you who is doing this."

Annabel's expression was icy. "I don't know where you're getting your information, but you don't know the details of this case."

He had crossed a line bringing up Matthew Colton, but the Coltons felt free to dig around in his life and in his business. Maybe they should get a taste of how it felt. "I get my information from the same screwed-up place everyone in this town goes for news. Rumors and gossip on Main Street."

"This isn't about my father. I am here to do my job." Her voice was low, but the ire in her eyes burned hot. She handed him the coffee mug. "I have the right to be on public property, and I would caution you to remember I am an officer of the law and I will arrest you if you try to impede me."

Jesse had rattled her, and while it wasn't his intention, he was irate, too. He could feel the hurt and fury shaking him. Regina wasn't a murderer. The Colton family turning their attention to her was akin to turning a blind eye to the real killer.

"Maybe the Coltons should spend time thinking about how close to home these murders are and how that might mean you're missing critical evidence. Blaming me and Regina is deflecting the real issue. A killer is stalking women in Granite Gulch, and you have no way to stop it."

Annabel had never been so furious with a person of interest in a case before. Her stomach was tight, and her skin felt hot. Jesse seemed comfortable turning the tables on her and shoving her family history in her face.

Her father was tied to this case, and Annabel was careful about that. She couldn't link the cases in her mind and see her father's behavior as Regina's. Her part in this case was minor, and letting Jesse drag her into a conversation about her father was nonproductive.

No one had ever spoken openly about her father. Her foster families, her classmates and her friends had talked about her father and what he had done behind her back. The few people she'd had a conversation with about Matthew and his crimes were gentle and sensitive, not asking too many questions or hurling accusations.

Was Jesse right? Did she have a blind spot when it came to the Alphabet Killer crimes? Every investigator was subject to their biases and their experiences. Her father's killings had shaped her life, in some ways for the better and in many ways, for the worse. But the police were following the facts and the evidence. It didn't matter what Annabel thought. The facts of what had happened and how they could stop the killer before she struck again were all that mattered.

Matthew Colton knew who the Alphabet Killer was, and he had pointed at Regina Willard. What the police and FBI had found in her boarding room in Rosewood had been damning. She had written the alphabet in a permanent red marker, a bull's-eye drawn beside each letter. News clippings of the killings and the victims had been posted on the wall. Were they missing parts of the story? It was a long shot, but could Regina be investigating the murders? Could she have stumbled on to facts about the case and, realizing she was a person of interest, started building her defense? She was tied to the case and the victims too closely to not be involved.

Annabel couldn't present Jesse with evidence in an ongoing investigation, but surely he saw the police were not making unfounded accusations. They had followed a process and the evidence.

A few months ago, before Regina Willard's name had come up in connection to the murders, Annabel had worried her sister, Josie, may have been the Alphabet Killer. Years before, Trevor had tried to gain custody of Josie, but Josie had refused to see her siblings or leave her foster home. When she was seventeen, Josie had disappeared. Her young fiancé had dumped her and had been seen kissing a woman with long dark hair. Long dark hair, like the victims of the Alphabet Killer.

With evidence mounting against Regina, Annabel had been thrilled to have a new lead and a new suspect. More than anything, Annabel wanted to reunite with her sister, and she didn't want it to be while she was slapping cuffs on her sister's wrists. Now it seemed Josie was in the clear, and yet she was still in the wind.

Had the FBI and police investigators made the leap to Regina as the Alphabet Killer too quickly without considering the case from every angle? As Annabel worked the facts over, every road led to Regina Willard. Jesse's denial didn't mean the police and FBI were wrong.

After staying at the farm until dark, Annabel sent a message to her boss and her brothers she was en route to Granite Gulch. Then she sent a message to Mia, asking to meet at her place and to bring reinforcements, that is, Mia's latest drool-worthy dessert. Annabel hadn't shaken the argument with Jesse from her thoughts, and she needed someone to talk to.

Her former foster sister and, in many ways, her

soul sister and biggest supporter, Mia Rivera worked at the Double G Cakes and Pies. She was talented in the kitchen and loved experimenting with treats and testing the results on Annabel.

Annabel had been alone with her thoughts for too long. Mia knew how to cheer her up. She could be honest without being brutal and wasn't afraid to call Annabel out when she was lying to herself or ignoring the truth.

When Annabel drove up to her house and saw her kitchen light on, her mood lifted. Mia had a key to Annabel's place. Annabel imagined the sweet smell of Mia's dessert, and she felt better knowing her dear friend would steer her in the right direction.

Talking to Mia was cheap therapy and ten times more effective. Annabel parked and trotted up the stairs. Her front door was locked, and she opened it with her key and called out to Mia.

Mia was in the kitchen reading a magazine Annabel had left on the counter. Annabel almost wept at the delicious smells filling the house. The tea kettle was heating on the stove. She hadn't anticipated how exhausting a stakeout would be. She was hungry, thirsty, cranky and tired.

"How am I this lucky to have a friend like you?" Annabel asked.

Mia grinned. "I feel the same way. I'm just paying you back for all those parking tickets you helped me fix."

There had been no parking tickets, but it was Mia's favorite joke.

"Now tell me what happened," Mia said, giving Annabel a hug.

Mia was warm and affectionate, a quality Annabel's brothers were lacking. She didn't blame them for their outward coolness. They had been raised in foster homes, and they had formed a tough outer shell in order to press through some of the more difficult problems in their lives. Annabel had seen cracks in Chris's facade from time to time, especially when he spoke of his late wife. At times, her brothers covered up deep, simmering emotions with jokes and banter.

Not that Annabel doubted they were sincere and warm inside. Zoe, Lizzie, Darcy and Laura were warm and compassionate women. They had to have broken through to Annabel's brothers and connected with them on a level Annabel hadn't.

Annabel pulled a barrette from her pocket and clipped an annoying strand of hair off her face. "I was given an actual assignment today, something meaningful and possibly helpful on a case. But a person of interest on that assignment asked me about my father."

Mia winced and pointed to the chair at the end of the table. "Sit. Tell me what was said."

Annabel recounted Jesse's words, adding her commentary. "I handled it terribly. I thought by now, I would have a stiff upper lip when Matthew is mentioned. But it rattled me."

Mia turned on the oven light and peeked inside. "That's understandable. Matthew Colton left your family a terrible legacy. When you first came to

Mama Jean's, you were sad and sullen. I had seen enough kids pass through I thought it was normal. But you also seemed scared. That was something different."

Mama Jean had been Annabel's first foster mother, and Annabel was thankful for her compassion and warmth and understanding every day. Without her, Annabel felt sure she wouldn't have coped with her mother's death and her father's atrocities. They were the darkest and saddest parts of Annabel's life, but Mama Jean had made living with those hurts possible.

Mama Jean had grown children of her own, and she had fostered what children she could. But she had provided more than a bed to sleep in and food to eat. She had taken time for Annabel, talked to her, drawn her out, let her grieve for her mother and the loss of her family, accepted her anger and countered it with love. Mama Jean had died of a stroke after a couple of years, and Annabel was sent to another foster home. She had learned the hard lesson that not all foster families were as loving.

At other homes, she was met with anger for displaying sadness. She was told to "smile" as if that did anything for the ache beneath her expression. Mama Jean had helped her press through the worst of her pain, and she had used the strength she had learned from her to get through rough times.

"It was a dark time for me. You and Mama Jean helped me, and I haven't forgotten that."

Wearing a pair of hot mitts Mia had gifted Annabel last Christmas, Mia pulled a pie from the oven.

"I know it. I'm the only woman in town who doesn't worry about speeding tickets." She winked at Annabel.

Mia had taken the place of the sister she had lost. Though Annabel often wondered what Josie was like or how her life had turned out, it eased the ache to have Mia.

Mia set the pie next to the kettle. Annabel grabbed mugs and her box of tea bags. "I feel bad for what I said to Jesse because he turned it around on me, and it hurt."

"Jesse? You're calling him by his first name?" Mia asked, interest lighting her voice.

"Yes. Is that bad?"

"Jesse Willard?"

Annabel hadn't meant to give away his identity. "That's him."

"He's come into the bakery a few times. Dead sexy. He's got that cowboy swagger and that borderline bad-boy attitude, like I could invite him to my place and do naughty things to him."

Annabel laughed. "I hadn't noticed how attractive he was."

"Almost knocked me down the first time he came into the shop. And when he spoke? He had that slow drawl, like he has all the time in the world and you're the only woman in it. I almost discreetly snapped his picture and messaged you, but that stuff with his sister is rough."

"He doesn't think she's guilty."

Mia made a face. "Then you know his flaw. He's delusional."

"Or in denial."

"In any case, neither is good. You don't want to go there. Complicated with a twist of confusing," Mia said. "And he questioned you about your father? Sounds like a defensive mechanism to avoid talking about his sister. You're the officer. He's the suspect. He answers questions, not asks them."

"Jesse isn't a suspect. He's a person of interest. I pushed him too hard. I wasn't supposed to talk to anyone on the assignment. I was supposed to watch and listen," Annabel said.

"Unless Chief Murray is clueless, which I know he is not, then he knew you'd get more involved than just watching," Mia said.

"Still, it was my first assignment. I should have handled it better. Jesse has me riled up."

"Because he's got insanity in his family tree?" Mia asked.

Neither she nor Mia could pretend their family trees weren't equally crazy. "He didn't seem unbalanced. He was controlled. He lost it when I pushed him, but otherwise, he was polite and calm."

"You're forgetting the most obvious part. The part where he is punch-in-the-ovaries gorgeous. I almost drooled into the desserts waiting on him. He called me ma'am, but it didn't sound like an old woman ma'am, more like an, 'I'd like to do wicked things to you and then treat you with respect in the morning.'"

Annabel laughed. "Mia, you're too much."

"Oh, come on, tell me every female part of your anatomy didn't stand up and take notice when you saw him."

The first moment when she had bumped into him in the precinct came to mind. She had taken notice. He was absolutely dreamy. "I'll admit it, but only to you. I will swear on a stack of Bibles I felt nothing—nothing—if one of my brothers asks."

"That's because they're overprotective. No way would they like you crushing on the brother of a serial killer."

"Alleged serial killer," Annabel said almost reflexively. But she was already thinking about Jesse's broad shoulders and trim waist, the way his jeans sat on his hips, and how she knew beneath those clothes were roped muscles and bronzed skin waiting for a woman's touch. He'd have a body hard won in the field, not in a gym, and that was more desirable.

"There's only one thing you can do," Mia said. "Besides sleep with him."

"I can't sleep with him! He's involved in a police and FBI investigation. And you just told me he's trouble."

"He is. Absolutely bound to get crazy and difficult. But that was before I saw your face. When you talk about him, you have stars in your eyes. I've seen that…never. If he's something special, regardless of the complexity, you need to act on it."

"I can't do anything about it. If Chief Murray finds out I'm crushing on Regina Willard's brother, he'll pull me from the assignment, and it may be years before he gives me another chance."

"Then don't tell Chief Murray anything. Write your reports and don't mention the sexy. This is Granite Gulch. There's, like, eight available, sexy men total, and you're related to almost half of them. And of those men, only Jesse Willard gets you hot and bothered."

Annabel laughed. "So I need to go for it because he's sexy and available and not related to me?"

"I'm not telling you to sneak into his bed and wait for him naked. I'm telling you to clear your conscience. This investigation will end eventually. It won't end well for him. Who better to understand what he's going through than someone who's been through it? Get back over there, patch things up and apologize."

"Apologize?" Annabel asked, though Mia was right. Annabel could have handled the situation better.

"You were in denial about your father for the longest time. You thought he was falsely imprisoned, or there had been a mistake."

Annabel recalled those feelings poignantly. "I couldn't resolve the person who I knew as my father with the monster the media was painting." Not that her father had been the picture of amazing. He'd rarely been stably employed, he'd fought with their mother, and he could be distant and cold.

"Mama Jean tried to shield you. She wouldn't let us watch television when the Matthew Colton case was on the news. But we found a way to follow the trial."

She and Mia had checked the newspapers in the library. Annabel hadn't understood most of what they'd read, but the longer the case had played out, the more Annabel had come to grips with what had happened. Accepting the incident had been a huge step to stopping the nightmares that had followed her after her mother had been killed. "How would I even approach him?"

"Take him an 'I'm sorry' gift, like some pie or a fruit basket, and tell him you understand what he's going through, and you appreciate his cooperation. Tell him you'll do what you can to respect his privacy, but you need to follow the leads in the case and do your job," Mia said.

She made it sound easy. "The more he cooperates and the faster we close the case, the better for him."

"And better for you," Mia said. "Keep it friendly, and you might snag a date to the spring festival." Mia walked to the stove and cut a piece of pie for each of them.

"I'll probably be working the festival," Annabel said.

"You don't work for three days straight. Stop building your own roadblocks."

Mia set two pieces of pie on the table. "Now try this pie and tell me what you like or don't like. It's a new recipe."

Annabel sat at the table, her shoulders feeling lighter. She knew what she had to do, and she would apologize. She could be the friend Jesse needed. She hadn't been involved with someone on a case before, but she could keep those boundaries straight, couldn't she?

Chapter 4

"Your brilliance inspires me. I've read everything, absolutely everything, you've written. Reporters scream you're a killer, but I know you had justifiable reasons for killing them. How much can one person take? How much pain and suffering can one person stand before they share that torment with others? Family causes the deepest pain, and it can make you want to kill them again and again and again."

Annabel set down the letter from Regina written to Matthew Colton. Most of her letters were similar in tone, worshipful of Matthew Colton and bitter about her life. Annabel hadn't spoken to Matthew Colton in years, and she didn't know exactly how he felt about the woman. Was he pleased by her ego stroking? Did he enjoy reading his fan mail?

Annabel was due to see him soon, and she would ask him about the letters. He may not answer her. Matthew Colton didn't do anything without gaining something in return. What could Annabel offer him? She couldn't spare his life. The cancer had laid claim to that. The little pull she had at the police precinct didn't extend to the prison.

Her father had collected a number of letters from strangers who had written him in jail. Some of his admirers had become long-term pen pals, and Annabel wondered what exactly Matthew wrote back to them. Words of encouragement? Advice on how to get away with murder? A certain type of individual wrote to inmates. Some did it for religious or spiritual reasons, believing they could help prisoners find God; others wanted to reach out as a kindness; but Regina and her ilk were another category entirely.

Obsessive and often suffering from their own mental diseases, they viewed the prisoner in the right and their crimes as achievements.

Matthew Colton was not remorseful about his actions. Time had not given him a fresh perspective. His children had not visited him in years, and Matthew hadn't seemed to care until recently.

Even on his deathbed, knowing the cancer would take his life, he hadn't repented. He didn't attend spiritual or religious services in prison.

Most of what Annabel knew about her father's murder spree was from the evidence the prosecutors had presented at his trial. Matthew hadn't explained to his children.

Whether he didn't know what to say or he didn't believe he owed his children an explanation, he had said nothing to them. No words of comfort or apologies. Nothing in the way of denying killing their mother or giving some reasons why he felt compelled to kill in ritualistic and sick acts.

Annabel couldn't remember those years in her life well. She couldn't recall her father speaking in anger about his victims, although Annabel remembered his anger for his brother, Big J. Big J had taken the brunt of Matthew's resentment, and Saralee Colton the rest of it.

Annabel's first memory was of her mother, her arms outstretched to her, and how good it felt to be wrapped in her warm and loving embrace. Her next clear memories were after their father had been arrested and the confusion that had followed. Annabel had wanted to know where their mother was, and no one would answer her. Strangers would look at her with pity and pat her shoulder, but no one would explain what had happened or why.

Mama Jean had clarified that her mother wasn't coming back. Annabel had wanted to tell her brothers, thinking she had discovered something they needed to know. She often wondered if she was the only sibling who hadn't grasped what had happened.

Or perhaps her coping mechanism had been to bury her head in the sand and wait for the brunt of the horror to pass.

Annabel put Regina Willard's and Matthew

Colton's letters back into the lockbox. The letters had not yielded any great understanding of her father.

"…kill them again and again and again."

Who thought like that? Regina's words haunted Annabel. Nothing in the letters their father had given them contained a confession from Regina. How had her father known Regina was the Alphabet Killer? Had he given the FBI all the letters? He could have destroyed some. Her father was a compulsive liar, and he wouldn't lose sleep over withholding information.

Matthew had nothing left to lose. He was dying in prison. Nothing could save him.

Annabel checked her front and back doors to ensure they were locked. A couple of times over the past months, Ridge and Lizzie had seen someone who looked like Josie peering in their windows. Annabel wondered if they had seen Regina Willard. The police believed Regina had been selecting her victims from the Blackthorn County All Night Diner. The credit card receipts from the diner were the only connection between the victims thus far. At least, the only connection Annabel had been made aware of.

Though killing the Coltons wouldn't fit with Regina's alphabet obsession, Annabel couldn't be sure Regina hadn't also formed an unhealthy fascination with Matthew Colton's children. Since objects of Regina's obsession were turning up dead, Annabel needed to be careful.

Annabel's service weapon was in her bedside table. She checked it was there and climbed into bed.

She was a professional and had studied disturbing cases in the police academy, but this case touched close to home. When she thought about Regina, she thought about Matthew Colton, and his name had a way of bringing unresolved problems to the surface. Maybe that's why she'd been having a hard time sleeping. Her father's letters from Regina made her feel watched and haunted and touched on something inside her that made her deeply uncomfortable.

Annabel lay down and waited for sleep to claim her.

She woke to the sound of creaking stairs. Had she dreamed the noise? Was it the house settling? She lived in an older home, and the groans of the wood shifting in the wind sometimes played tricks on her.

She was hot and sweaty, and she reached into her side table for her gun. Her shirt was sticking to her body, and her hair was damp against her neck. Checking the safety, she climbed out of bed and pressed her body against the wall of her bedroom behind the door. She shivered, the sweat on her skin making her cold. If she called 911 or one of her brothers and it was a false alarm, she wouldn't live it down. New to the police force or not, she could hold her own. She was trained to use her weapon.

After several minutes passed without hearing another noise, she checked the bedrooms and the bathroom. Finding them empty, she took the stairs to the first floor. The front door was locked and bolted. The windows were closed and latched. The house was empty.

It had been her imagination. Breathing a sigh of

relief, she was too keyed up to return to sleep. She turned on the television in the living room and sat on the sofa. She could have put her gun away, but she felt safer with it close. She threw a blanket over her lap.

Too many times, she had imagined what her father's and Regina's victims must have felt like at the end of their lives. She imagined the terror they experienced, perhaps regret or anger. As Annabel flipped through the television stations, she thought again of Regina's letters.

Did Regina have an ax to grind with her family? She'd written she understood why someone would want to kill a family member. Did that mean Jesse? Was he in danger? All of Regina's known victims had been women. Could Regina be targeting her brother, too? What was her ultimate plan? If she was trying to impress Matthew Colton, how would she feel to learn he was dying?

It was not a secret Matthew's life was ending. How looped in was Regina? If she hoped to complete the alphabet's worth of killings before Matthew died, she might increase her pace.

Jesse seemed incapable of believing his sister was a murderer. That was a dangerous stance to take. If Regina showed up at his farm, he'd let her inside his house. He might encourage her to go to the police to talk to them, but what good would that do if she killed him?

Annabel had to warn Jesse. She didn't make her best decisions at three in the morning. She would tell the chief her theory tomorrow and see how he handled it. Jesse could be in denial about his sister, but he should be aware he may be the killer's next bull's-eye.

After about an hour, knowing she would be tired at work again tomorrow, Annabel crawled back into bed, setting her gun down, safety on. She would sleep easier when the Alphabet Killer was caught and she had visited Matthew Colton, obligation fulfilled.

Annabel would have closure and move on with her life.

"Mistake number one. You can't let a civilian see you get upset," Luis said, turning their police cruiser onto Main Street.

He had returned from his minivacation, and the time away from the job seemed to have taken the edge off his annoyance with their mundane assignments. After her brief flirtation with working an active and dangerous investigation, she and Luis were patrolling the streets. She was filling him in on what he'd missed. The most exciting event of the past couple of days had been her fireworks with Jesse. Annabel was careful to keep her tone neutral and not give away that some of those fireworks had to do with her feelings for Jesse.

Main Street was more crowded than usual, with the setup for the town fair, the Spring Fling, underway. Local farmers would bring their registration sheets for weekly deliveries and fresh produce to persuade more townspeople to sign up. Produce stands would offer fresh fruits and vegetables for a great price. Musicians would play, people who knew how would line dance and anyone who had something to sell would be there. It was a town-wide event, and almost everyone would make an appearance.

Would Regina?

"I wish I could have seen my face when he was talking to me," Annabel said. "I thought I was keeping it together, but now I'm not sure." At least she hadn't had a totally overemotional reaction and cried or punched Jesse. After taking a couple days to cool off, she had mentally composed her apology and would see him as soon as possible to deliver it.

Annabel did a double take when she spotted a familiar face loping down the sidewalk. "Luis, that's the guy! That's one of the men who beat our vic senseless and then ran."

The moment the car stopped, Annabel was in pursuit. The suspect was strolling along the sidewalk, appearing bored.

He must have heard her pounding footsteps behind him, because he turned. She had hoped to grab him before he saw her coming.

"Police! Stop and show me your hands!" Annabel yelled.

Luis was three feet behind her. They chased the suspect, and when Annabel was close enough, she launched her body into his, knocking him against the Dairy and Creamery. She rolled onto her feet, and the victim swung at her with his left fist. She leaned away and avoided the blow, but his right caught her cheek.

Annabel was dazed. Regrouping, she hit him hard

across the face and once in the gut, sending him doubling over in pain.

Luis was at her side, and he wrestled the man to the ground. He pulled the suspect's arms behind his back and snapped handcuffs on his wrists.

"You're under arrest," Annabel said, catching her breath and giving him his Miranda rights.

Luis dragged the victim to his feet. "Pat him down?" he asked, holding the victim's arms firmly.

"Do you have any needles or knives?" she asked. Before she checked his pockets she needed to know.

The man didn't respond.

Luis shook him. "She asked you a question."

"I may have some medical equipment in my pockets," the perp said.

They walked the suspect to their police car. Annabel pulled on a pair of gloves and grabbed an evidence bag from their street kit.

Annabel carefully reached into the side pocket of his cargo pants and withdrew what looked like heroin and a used needle. She dropped both into the evidence bag. She checked his other pockets and found a handgun. "I hope you have a license to carry a concealed weapon."

The look on his face indicated he did not, and Annabel guessed they would find the gun was registered to someone else, possibly reported stolen.

Annabel pulled his wallet from his back pocket. She opened it and looked at the driver's license. "Dylan Morris."

Dylan grunted.

They put Dylan in the back of the squad car and headed toward the police station.

"You'll be sorry for doing this," Dylan said.

Annabel said nothing. She wasn't sorry. She was pleased Dylan had been stupid enough to return to Main Street close to the scene of the beating. A smarter criminal would have skipped town and waited it out. Other cases would have moved front and center, and Annabel's memory of the event would have faded.

"You're making a big mistake," Dylan said.

"Shut up, pal," Luis said. "You can work it out with your court-appointed attorney."

Dylan grumbled and leaned back in the seat. "You have no right to arrest me. I wasn't doing anything wrong."

"You not only assaulted a police officer, but you also match the description of a man I saw at a crime scene a few days ago. Don't you remember us? Did you think we would forget you so quickly?" Annabel asked.

Dylan muttered something about stupid cops, and Annabel ignored him. He was making it worse for himself, and Annabel wouldn't let him get under her skin.

"Nice work spotting him," Luis said.

It wasn't a huge compliment, but coming from Luis, it was something. They pulled into the station and parked.

"I want my phone call," Dylan said.

"You'll get it," Annabel said, pulling him from the back of their squad car.

She led him into the police station, feeling publicly accomplished for the first time in her career. She had found the man who'd run from the scene of the beating.

Annabel and Luis handed off Dylan to the detective who'd caught the case of the alley beating.

"Hey, Annabel, Luis." Sam jogged over to them as they were leaving the precinct. "Nice job with that." Sam nodded his head in Dylan's direction.

She could have made a snarky comment about how she and Luis were good at catching criminals when they were allowed to do their jobs, but she answered with a smile. "Thank you."

Sam shifted on his feet. "I received a call about a female shooting victim, who is on her way to the hospital, but may be able to tell us something about the shooter," Sam said.

Us? Big week. Annabel had been involved with a stakeout, an arrest and now a shooting victim.

She and Luis followed Sam to his car, and they climbed inside. Sam turned on his lights and sirens. Granite Gulch wasn't a hot spot for murders. They had far more vehicular and accidental deaths than they did homicides.

Sam peeled out of the parking lot heading north. "This case could be one of the Alphabet Killer murders. We have not confirmed, and we're not telling the media anything yet. We don't want an unnecessary panic. We're short officers, and I know we're not the chief's first pick. Annabel is familiar with the letters from Matthew. I'm interested if anything jumps out about what the victim says. Maybe we've been missing a key piece of evidence."

Sam pressed harder on the accelerator. "We'll go to the scene after we speak to the victim, but only to observe. The FBI is processing it."

Annabel had to keep some distance between herself and this case. Being asked for her opinion was flattering. "What do you know about the shooting?"

"The victim's name is Gwendolyn Johnson. She called 911. Paramedics were the first on the scene. She was shot twice in the chest."

Sam made the thirty-minute drive to the hospital in twenty. They pulled into the ER parking area, taking the spots reserved for the police, and hurried inside. The waiting area was crowded, and the admissions desk had a long line.

Sam raced to the front of the line and held up his badge. "Detective Sam Colton with the Granite Gulch Police Department. A gunshot victim was brought in about twenty minutes ago, and we need to talk to her."

A bored-looking administrator with spiral curls wearing pink scrubs lifted her eyebrow. "Sir, you need to wait in line."

Annabel looked around for Darcy. She was an ER doctor, and if she was working, she would help them the best she could. No sign of her.

The look on Sam's face was apoplectic. "You need to tell me where she is."

A nurse came around the corner. "Are you here about Gwendolyn Johnson?"

Sam nodded, and the nurse gestured for them to follow her. "Your chief called to tell us you'd be coming in. Gwendolyn is being prepped for surgery."

"I need to speak with her," Sam said.

The nurse held out her hand. "The patient is medicated, and when the OR is prepped, she's headed immediately into surgery. I don't know if she'll be capable of answering your questions."

Annabel stepped forward. "Please, she's the only surviving victim in a series of murders. She might have valuable information we need to stop her attacker."

The nurse's eyes went wide. "I saw the red circles on her forehead, and I wondered. Wait here. I'll talk to the doctor."

The nurse disappeared for a few minutes.

Annabel felt her anxiety tick up a few notches. Anything could happen now. Gwendolyn could provide them with the greatest lead they'd ever had, or she could tell them nothing.

The nurse hurried back to them. "You," she said pointing to Annabel. "You can speak to her. Two minutes. No more."

Annabel didn't waste time confirming with Luis and Sam that it was okay or why she was selected— maybe because she was a woman or her demeanor was calmer than the other officers'. Sam pressed a voice recorder and a picture into Annabel's hand. Annabel glanced at it. It was a picture of Regina Willard, her hair mussed, her eyes wide and wild, and her mouth turned down into a frown. Knowing what she had done and knowing who she was, Annabel felt a tremor of disgust and fear. Despite the manhunt for Regina, she had evaded them. She was not to be underestimated.

Annabel raced to Gwendolyn's bedside. Gwendolyn had red marker on her forehead in the shape of a bull's-eye, the dot slightly off center. Her eyes were closed.

"Gwendolyn?" Annabel flipped on the voice recorder. Annabel's connection to the case via her father meant everything had to be aboveboard. She couldn't leave openings for a defense lawyer to shred their evidence.

The woman's eyes opened into slits.

Annabel was excited and anxious, but she kept herself calm, hoping not to rile Gwendolyn. Gwendolyn had been through a trauma, and she was fading. "My name is Officer Annabel Colton. Can you tell me anything about the person who shot you?" If she had two minutes, she had to get to the point.

Gwendolyn's medical equipment beeped rhythmically and the lights were green, but she'd closed her eyes again.

"I know you're tired and this isn't what you want to talk about now, but we want to find and stop this person. Anything you can tell me will help."

Gwendolyn opened her eyes. "She said, 'who's the big shot now?' I fell."

Annabel tried to picture the scene and hoped the

evidence the FBI collected, along with details Gwendolyn was providing, would build a clear picture of the incident. Every scrap could lead to Regina's arrest.

"She wrote on my face. I thought she would leave. But she got to the front door, she turned around and shot me again."

Regina hadn't robbed any of her victims. Her sole reason for attacking these women was some distorted sense of revenge, as if whatever had happened between Regina and her victims justified them being killed. "Do you know the woman who shot you?"

Gwendolyn didn't answer for several long beats. The medication might have put her to sleep. "Yes. The woman on the news. The Alphabet Killer."

Annabel hated to put Gwendolyn through this, but she wanted to build the strongest case possible. She held up the picture of Regina Willard. "Does this woman look familiar to you?"

Gwendolyn opened her eyes and moaned. "That's her. That's the woman who shot me."

Her medical monitors began beeping incessantly and loudly, lines and buttons flashing red. Doctors and nurses rushed into the room. Annabel stepped out into the hallway to give them space to work.

Sam and Luis were pacing and ran to her side. "What did she say?" Luis asked.

Annabel turned off the voice recorder and handed it to Sam. "I recorded everything. But the most critical part was she positively IDed Regina Willard. She's the Alphabet Killer, and we finally have a witness who lived long enough to confirm it."

Sam, Luis and Annabel returned the recorded evidence to the GGPD and then drove to Gwendolyn's home. The entire house had been searched for evidence, and FBI crime-scene techs were analyzing the scene, collecting hair and fingerprints. Though the positive ID was helpful, to build their case, they needed solid forensic evidence.

A clever defense lawyer could claim the ID was the delusion of a medicated woman or that the police had forced Gwendolyn to make an ID outside of a proper lineup.

"The chief wants us to look at the scene. See if anything jumps out at you from reading the letters. Do not touch anything. If we see something, we need to report it to the FBI, and they will look deeper into it," Sam said.

The FBI was spearheading the investigation, and the GGPD were assisting. They knew the locals and the town better, and Chief Murray was insistent they be as helpful and accommodating as possible. He wasn't acting territorial. Everyone knew the case was a matter of life and death. The faster they could catch Regina, the fewer the victims.

Sam led her and Luis around the back of the house. "They believe the killer entered through the back door and exited through the front." The glass was broken on the door's glass panes. If Regina had reached inside to unlock the door, she could have left DNA evidence.

They circled the house slowly. When they reached the front door, they slid cloth booties over their shoes and pulled gloves on to their hands. They entered. This was Annabel's first attempted murder scene. Large puddles of blood pooled on the floor, and the house looked trashed, as if an altercation had taken place. Gwendolyn hadn't mentioned struggling with Regina.

"Two gunshot wounds?" Annabel asked.

"That's what it looks like."

Trevor walked into the room and lifted his hand in greeting to his siblings. "See anything?"

"Just arrived," Sam said.

"We found the gun casings. We'll run them through ballistics," Trevor said.

They'd try to match them to the other scenes. "Was there a struggle?" Annabel asked.

Trevor looked around the room. "I think Regina flew into a rage when the house was empty. She selected Gwendolyn Johnson as her target. Gwendolyn arrived home, and Regina was waiting."

Annabel looked around the small home. "Regina doesn't work at the diner any longer. Where is she meeting her victims? How does she know Gwendolyn?"

Annabel flinched when she saw two pillows on the couch with the initials *G* and *J*. Gwendolyn Johnson. The *G* pillow had red circle inked on to it, the bull's-eye stamped over the letter.

"We'll talk to Gwendolyn's family and friends and try to figure out where she works and where she shops and visits. Maybe we can make a connection," Trevor said.

They would check Gwendolyn's credit card records to see where she had eaten and gone in the past several days. She had to have crossed paths with Regina Willard, which would give them some indication of where Regina was hiding.

Annabel had hoped after they'd tracked Regina to Rosewood, she would realize they were close to finding her, and she would lie low. But it seemed she was bent on taking more victims, returning to Granite Gulch and following in Matthew's footsteps.

It had taken the authorities years to find and stop Mathew Colton. How many lives would Regina Willard claim before she was found?

Chapter 5

Armed with her well-rehearsed apology and a cup of her favorite coffee from the Java Hut, Annabel pulled into the driveway leading to Jesse's farm. This wasn't a professional visit. She saw no need to park on the street and walk the eighth of a mile to the house.

Posted on the barn was the sign for Willard's Farm. Ten years ago, when it had been Old Man Ridley's place, it had been a run-down mess.

Jesse Willard had been working hard to make it a productive farm. Regina was bent on destruction, and based on the details of her life the police were piecing together, she was a mess, skipping from job to job, town to town. The FBI had found few significant boyfriends or friends whom she'd formed long-term relationships with. She had developed an obsession with Matthew Colton, her ex-fiancé and, Annabel guessed, any number of unhealthy other people. Annabel wasn't sure if Regina was seeking the infamy Matthew Colton had, or she felt her actions were justified because Matthew had committed similar crimes.

Annabel took the tray of coffee from the passenger seat, the two cups set diagonal from each other. They smelled great. Who didn't like coffee from the Java Hut? It was quiet on the farm except for the tick of the irrigation system as it sprayed the fields. The farmhands must have been finished for the day. It was about an hour until dusk.

Annabel opened her car door, balancing the tray in one hand and slipping her keys into her pocket with the other. The sound of gunshots had her reaching for the weapon she realized she wasn't carrying. She was off duty and had chosen to leave it home, trying to present herself as friendly and open. Big mistake to come to the farm unarmed.

Hunters in the area, or was she under attack? A bullet pierced her window, answering that question.

She dropped the coffee, and the liquid burned her through her jeans. She dove back into the car, squatting low in the driver's seat well. Her back window broke, glass raining into the backseat. That pissed her off almost as much as being shot at. She had bought this car years before, and it was old, but it was hers.

Annabel pulled her phone from the cup holder and called the police. "Off- duty police officer at Willard's Farm. Shots fired."

Who was shooting at her? Regina Willard? Someone after Jesse? It had crossed her mind that Regina's rantings could point to Jesse as a target. How did Regina feel about Jesse and his mother leaving Regina and her father? Abandonment could create a profound sense of betrayal. Those wounds could cut deep. Jesse had been a child at the time, but Regina could view being left with her father in a dozen different ways. Regina seemed fine playing the role of the victim. She seemed to have plenty of blame to spread around.

In her letters, she wrote about being left by her fiancé. About being done wrong by others. About being raised by a monster, who'd shredded her self-esteem.

The last place Annabel should be was inside her car. The shooting had stopped. The shooter could be working his or her way around to the car and have her penned in. The phrase "shooting fish in a barrel" came to mind, and Annabel knew she needed to move. She would be exposed as she fled the car, but staying inside was more dangerous. She needed to protect Jesse and anyone else on the farm, or at least warn them of trouble.

Annabel slipped out of the passenger side of the car, staying low, hitting her knee on the emergency brake. She waited a beat, then crawled toward Jesse's house.

Jesse opened the front door and stood on the porch. Panic rose up inside her. If the shooter was targeting Jesse, he was in the open, and a decent marksman could make the kill shot without much trouble.

"Get down!" Annabel screamed, rushing at him and trying to cover him with her body. She stumbled up the steps, her adrenaline pulsing hard. She shoved him back inside the house, and they toppled over each other, Jesse catching her before she hit the ground. She kicked the door closed with her foot.

Lying on top of him, she met his gaze, and her entire body shuddered with desire. "There's a shooter," she said, perhaps stating the obvious but feeling as if she needed to provide a reason for why she had tackled him.

He smelled good, like mint and earth. Realizing she was in an intimate position, she rolled to the side, moving off him.

"Are you sure it's not a hunter?" Jesse asked.

"A hunter of people, sure," Annabel said. She came to her feet and crouched by the front window to watch for movement in the distance or even to catch a glimpse of the shooter. "Someone was shooting at me, bullets coming toward my car and your house."

Jesse had left the room, but she heard his footsteps and turned to see him returning with a rifle. She felt no danger from him, despite the anger in his eyes. "I don't know what this is about, but I'll defend you and my property."

"Do you have any staff on the premises who need to be warned?"

"Grace left about thirty minutes ago. She was the last to go."

"Grace?" Not important at the moment, but Annabel wondered about the woman she had seen with Jesse the other day.

"She's a farmhand. Works in the house sometimes."

Jesse was looking out the window, standing to the left of it. "Check the back door. Make sure it's locked."

Annabel did as he asked, surprised at how neat and tidy the house was. The decor was too masculine and plain for her tastes, but it was updated and modern. Jesse had put work into his home as well as the farm. She checked the doors and windows and returned to the front room.

Annabel stood next to Jesse, pressing herself against the wall. "Everything is locked. I called for assistance. We need to wait this guy out."

The window in front of them shattered, and Jesse pivoted toward her, covering her with his body. "Are you okay? Are you cut?"

She was fine. "I should be protecting you," she said. Their eyes held, and heat sizzled between them.

Annabel shifted in her jeans. She had taken more care than usual with her outfit to appear sophisticated and professional, but having him close, something in his assessing stare made her feel naked.

She touched the side of his face. "You've been cut." She reached to the console table along the wall and grabbed a box of tissues. She took one and dabbed at his cheek.

"It's okay. I'm fine," he said.

He peered out the window. "I don't see anyone. Where is this psycho shooting from?"

Across from the house were fields, but the crops were lower to the ground this time of year, not tall enough for someone to hide. Past the fields were a copse of trees.

"The trees." They spoke the words at the same time.

"No way of getting closer and staying under cover," Annabel said. "We'll have to wait for backup."

"It will take the police at least twenty minutes to get here," he said. "By then, it will be dark, and the shooter will be gone. Since he didn't accomplish what he set out to do, he'll be back," Jesse said.

"What do you think he set out to do?" Annabel asked.

"Kill you or kill me," Jesse said.

Annabel started. "This is your place. Why would someone target me? I wasn't followed here." If Regina was targeting her brother, she may have shot at Annabel as a matter of convenience. Certainly, Regina knew law enforcement wasn't on her side. She was a wanted woman.

"Someone could have followed you without you knowing. Then again, I get plenty of dirty looks from people who think my sister is the Alphabet Killer. Maybe that's what this is about."

It was on the tip of her tongue to tell him about Gwendolyn Johnson, but this wasn't the right time. Mama Jean had been patient and kind in helping Annabel to understand what her father had done. Being slammed in the face with facts wasn't passing on that same kindness. "We don't know if the shooter is finished or if he is looking for another attack point."

"Your leg. Are you bleeding?" Jesse asked, kneeling on the floor, taking her calf in his hands and examining it.

She shook her head. "Not blood. Coffee. I brought you some coffee from the Java Hut."

He inclined his head. "Why?"

Annabel looked out the window. Still no one moving toward the house from that direction. "I wanted to apologize."

He released her leg and stood. "For?"

He wasn't making this easy for her. "For the other day. For asking you those questions when I wasn't prepared to answer them myself." She hadn't been told to question him, and she should have kept her mouth shut. What she knew about the case wasn't important.

Jesse nodded once swiftly. She read something akin to respect in his eyes. "Apology accepted. I didn't help matters by getting defensive about Regina. When someone comes after my family, I get prickly."

"I do the same," Annabel said. "I have four brothers. They get on my nerves sometimes, but I don't let anyone talk badly about them."

They'd reached an understanding, and that was good enough for now.

"Let's go upstairs. We can get a better view of the farm from the bedrooms."

He meant nothing except providing a way to protect themselves, but Annabel's body tingled with excitement. Jesse's bedroom. She was reading into this, letting a tiny piece of her imagination run to a place where she and Jesse were intimate.

It had been too long since Annabel had been in a relationship. Her adrenaline was firing, and she was keyed up, thinking about Jesse in a sexual context when she needed to be focused on keeping them safe.

They took the stairs quickly, and Jesse pointed down the hall. "Stay low. Watch from that side. I'll get this side."

From her post in what she assumed was the guest bedroom, she could see clear across Jesse's land. It was a nice piece of property, rolling green and beautiful views. "What made you decide to become a farmer?" she called down the hall.

"Is this more of the interrogation, or are you passing the time?" He sounded as if he was teasing. It was a step in the right direction that they could joke with each other, and every word wasn't taken as an insult.

"Just a distraction. I'll holler if I see anyone."

"I've worked the land in some manner or another most of my adult life. I was tired of working for someone else, taking seasonal work for crappy pay. I saved my pennies and started planning. I decided I would buy a farm and run it the way I wish other farms had been run. I wanted my employees to be more than hourly wages on the books. When this place became available, I knew, with some elbow grease, it could shine. I bought it, and I haven't looked back."

A movement out of the corner of her eye had her spinning around, poised to attack. She let out a whistle. It was a cat. The black-and-white-spotted cat strolled across the room, watching her. "Your cat just took nine years off my life," Annabel said.

"Meet Diva. She showed up here last Halloween. First and last cat I let come in the house. She doesn't like the barn."

The cat walked toward Annabel and rubbed up against her leg. "She's touching me. Is that good?"

"She's letting you know she's the woman of the house. As long as you accept that, you'll be great friends."

Annabel bent to pat her side. "I know my place. It's okay, Diva." Annabel checked the windows again, not happy to see the sun fading. Darkness gave the shooter cover to move closer. If he or she was smart, waiting for the right time to strike again was no big deal.

The cat scampered away and perched on a purple pad set on the bed. "Is that where you sleep?" Annabel asked the cat over her shoulder.

The cat purred and laid her head on the pad and closed her eyes.

A curse from down the hall.

"What's wrong?" Annabel called, her heart thumping hard. She would feel better if she were armed. She hadn't before used her gun in the line of duty, but having it close made her feel secure. To protect herself or others, she would use it as she had been trained. "Do you see the shooter?"

"No sign of anyone. But my dogs are outside. Beau and Domino. They usually stay in the barn, but it's dinnertime. I need to let them in. What if the shooter takes aim at them?" Worry and fear underscored every word.

"The shooter has no reason to harm your dogs," Annabel said, but not knowing anything about the attacker, she had no way of telling what the shooter's intentions were. "We'll open the door carefully. Which door?"

"They'll come to the back door."

Annabel entered Jesse's bedroom. "I'll watch the front. Go. Be careful."

He nodded and hurried down the stairs to let his dogs inside. She heard their happy barking and then Jesse closing the door. He was talking to them, telling them he was happy they were safe, and pouring food into bowls.

What a charming man, with his work ethic and kindness to his pets and his thoughtfulness with his farmhands. How could this man be related to Regina Willard? From everything the police had gathered about Regina, she was a sick and twisted woman.

The crime scene at Gwendolyn Johnson's house snapped to mind, and Annabel shivered. Selecting victims based on their first names and a generic description matching almost any woman was disturbing. Being able to explain why a crime had occurred made citizens feel better. Even saying "the murders happened at night" or "only happened to people criminally involved with the murderer" was something to help people rest easy. But aside from the bull's-eye on their foreheads and the physical similarities of the victims, the crime scenes were different.

The police believed Regina selected her victims based on their names and a perceived mistreatment by them. But despite the extensive media coverage of the murders, they had not received any credible leads on Regina. She would think most brunettes in the area were wary of anyone matching Regina's description and would either avoid them or be kind. Unless the police could find Regina soon, Annabel was waiting for the news that another victim, a brunette whose named started with *H*, had been found, shot and left with a bull's-eye on her forehead.

Annabel crawled to the side window and peered out, watching for movement. If the shooter was looking at the house, he could be waiting to take his shot. Annabel wouldn't give him a head shot. The lower the sun set in the sky, the more shadows fell over the area. They hadn't spotted the shooter, and Annabel had nothing to provide the police in the way of a physical description. The likelihood of seeing anything now was slim.

Annabel glanced around the room. Jesse's bedroom wasn't what she expected. Like the rest of the house, it was painted in warm neutrals, the brown wood furniture sturdy and serviceable, but not overly large for the room. Missing from the room were pictures and personal items. No family photos or knickknacks on the tops of dressers. The bed was neatly made with a tan bedspread, and while it looked comfortable, he had two pillows, one on each side of the bed. The curtains were white, allowing in what remained of the sun.

Did Jesse use both of those pillows? One for himself and one for a girlfriend? If he had a girlfriend, she hadn't put her feminine touch on the room or the house in general. Before Annabel could imagine the changes she would make to the house if she was Jesse's, the sounds of police sirens filled the air, and relief washed over her.

The cavalry had arrived. Now she and Jesse stood a fighting chance.

The peaceful life Jesse had hoped to carve out for himself on his farm was rapidly becoming a fantasy. He didn't want to face accusations and deal with murders and shootings. He wanted to work his land and be left alone. While he was cordial and polite to other farmers in the area and even attended a yearly holiday party at one of his neighbors' farms, he held people at a distance.

It didn't take a psychologist or therapy sessions for him to realize he kept people away because his childhood had been a mess. His father was a terrible person, and Jesse had spent more time tending to his mother than she had caring for him.

Jesse hadn't been proud of the life he'd led, and, therefore, he didn't make friends easily or want anyone around discovering how crappy his life had been. Jesse didn't dwell on the past, but he had made promises to himself about the future. He would be a man others were happy to call a friend. He would take pride in his home and not be embarrassed for someone to see it.

When he and his mother had left his father and Regina, they'd had no money. About fourteen dollars. It had been long, hard nights on the run until Jesse had found a job stocking shelves at a food store. He'd lied about his age to get the job. It had been stable work and a decent paycheck. The owner of the store had even turned his back when Jesse sifted through the expired foods for something to eat.

Jesse's life now was miles better than it had been as a child. A few close friends, a job he loved and available food in spades.

The Granite Gulch police and the FBI arrived, their sirens screaming. Jesse lived far enough from town that the sirens would only accomplish scaring away the shooter. It wasn't as though this far out, the authorities had to worry about navigating through traffic.

He and Annabel left his house. He wanted to know what was happening on his farm. The shooter could have damaged other places on the farm, vandalized something or harmed his animals. The idea incensed him.

"Where are you going?" Annabel asked.

Suspicion had returned to her voice, and that quickly, the camaraderie they had formed splintered. "I am not going to talk to Regina. I need to check on my animals. If someone shot at me, he could have taken out his anger on them."

Annabel's jaw slackened. "I wasn't accusing you of anything. It is not safe for you to walk around the farm until we've checked the area."

He felt bad for jumping to the worst conclusion about her. "Then come with me. You're the police."

"I don't have my weapon."

He lifted his shotgun. "I have mine."

Annabel jogged over to his side. "Lead the way. Eyes open."

As they walked to the barn, Jesse prayed his animals were safe. The only animals that seemed upset were his horses. Though they had not been physically injured in the shooting, they were sensitive to loud noises, especially ones they were not accustomed to. His horses were also perceptive. They had sensed the danger.

Jesse calmed them, taking time to talk to each one, to pat and stroke them. When he was satisfied they were calm and would sleep, he and Annabel returned to the main house.

His dogs were barking at the windows, excited by the unfamiliar people on the premises.

A man in plainclothes—Jesse didn't know if he was police or FBI—addressed Annabel and Jesse. "We've found shell casings and bullets at the base of some nearby trees. No signs of the shooter."

"Do you believe Regina is the shooter?" Jesse asked the question plainly. Dancing around it would make it seem as if he had something to hide. Knowing the scope of the trouble his sister was in was important to him. Helping her get out of it was even more crucial.

The man remained taciturn. "We're considering all angles at the moment. We'll know more when we process the scene."

The shooter was not Regina because Regina

wouldn't shoot at him. "I hope you can rule her out from the evidence, because she didn't do this."

Annabel touched Jesse's sleeve. "We're ruling you out as a suspect."

As if that made it better. It was ludicrous to think he had done this or been part of any shooting in Granite Gulch. His shotgun was for protection, mainly from animal predators who may try to kill his chickens.

Jesse folded his arms over his chest. He had thought he and Annabel had made a real connection, but now, she was back to playing cop and suspect with him. "It would be hard to shoot at myself and my home since I was with you at the time."

Annabel winced. "I didn't mean it that way. I'm sure you're upset. This whole situation is distressing."

"I was a suspect in the shooting, though, wasn't I?" Maybe not in her mind, but the police had likely considered it.

"I knew it wasn't you."

The man was watching the exchange, his eyes narrowed as if scrutinizing their every word.

"You knew it wasn't me because you saw me coming out of the house." Was that the only reason? Was he such a despicable person in her eyes that she could picture him shooting at her? Shooting at anyone? For a depressing moment, Jesse wondered if he gave off the stink of being a monster. His father had it. Maybe he'd passed it to Jesse, and no matter how hard he worked to be a good person, everyone would believe he was a repugnant man.

Annabel shook her head. "Even before you exited the house, I hadn't considered it was you."

He sensed she was telling the truth, and his growing self-doubt dissipated. Maybe he could escape the past.

"Tell me again why you were here, Officer Colton," the man said.

Annabel swallowed hard. She glanced at Jesse and then faced the other man. "I exchanged unpleasant words with Mr. Willard the other day, and I came to apologize."

"That wasn't in your report," the man said.

"It had nothing to do with Regina," Annabel said.

"That's not for you to decide. We can discuss it later," the man said. Someone called to "chief," and the man turned. "Excuse me."

As he strode away, Annabel ran her hand over her face. "That was bad."

"Your chief?" Jesse asked, confirming.

"Chief Murray. He gave me the assignment to watch the farm for Regina. I crossed a line when I talked to you."

"I didn't mean to get you into trouble," Jesse said.

Annabel sighed. "You didn't. I came here because I was trying to make positive ties to the community and prevent any hostility from forming. I'll need to make it clear to Chief Murray that there's nothing between us."

Saying they had nothing between them felt like a punch in the gut. "Nothing?" Jesse asked. One word, but it felt needy and desperate. He regretted speaking it.

She looked at the ground, and when she lifted her eyes to meet his, he read her confusion. "You're the brother of a suspect in an active investigation."

"A suspect. Regina isn't guilty."

"I'm not supposed to get involved with anyone on the case. I'm already Matthew Colton's daughter, which is bad enough. I can't muddy the water by being involved with you."

The way she said it, it was as if she was considering the possibility of them being more than "nothing."

"I understand where you're coming from." Being related to Regina created complications for him, as well.

Annabel looked as if she wanted to say something more. "Let me help you clean up the glass."

A pointed change in the subject, and he didn't pursue the conversation about Regina. He didn't want to argue with Annabel about it. He only hoped the police would find the person who had shot at Annabel today and perhaps find the individual was the Alphabet Killer, too.

"I need to grab some boards to cover up the windows until I can order replacement glass," Jesse said.

"I'll give you a hand."

Annabel followed him to the barn, where he had sheets of plywood and spare wood from other renovation projects. Lifting one side with Annabel on the other, they walked the sheets to the house.

Setting the wood on the porch, he grabbed his

broom and dustpan. Annabel extended her hand for the broom. She started sweeping.

"I hope you'll consider this part of my apology," Annabel said. "I am sorry for speaking to you unprofessionally."

He hadn't expected an apology. People in positions of authority rarely admitted when they were wrong or when they had crossed a line. Though he understood why Annabel had questioned him, he appreciated she knew she had pushed hard and far.

Annabel and her brothers would see they were pointing their fingers at the wrong woman.

Chapter 6

While Annabel swept broken glass from the floor, Jesse nailed the boards over the windows. They worked in companionable silence. With the police milling around the house, asking her personal questions could land her in trouble, and he didn't want to talk about the Alphabet Killer.

His mind wandered to the list of tasks he had to do before he went to bed. "I'll need to call my staff and let everyone know there was a shooter on the farm," Jesse said. They would need to be careful and watch out for each other extra closely.

"Do you think anyone on your staff has a bone to pick with you?" Annabel asked.

The question jolted him. It must be hard to see criminals everywhere. Jesse had known a lot of bad people in his life, but he believed people were mostly good. His staff was well paid, and Jesse didn't expect more than an honest eight hours of work per day. Bad employees were few and far between, and part of that was his carefulness in hiring. Not that he hadn't made mistakes. "All things considered, I've been lucky. I can only think of one employee who left on bad terms. I had to fire him. He didn't show up on time, he didn't complete his tasks, and while I can't prove it, he came to work high or drunk a few times. Can't have that around farm equipment and animals. Someone could get hurt or worse."

Annabel had stopped sweeping and was looking at him. "Did you give the police his name?"

Annabel had been the first to ask about former or current problematic employees. "Dylan Morris."

Annabel inhaled sharply but said nothing.

"Someone you know?" Jesse asked.

"I don't know him personally," Annabel said.

Then perhaps Dylan had a rap sheet well known around the GGPD. "I wouldn't be surprised if he was tangled up in more problems. He doesn't make the best decisions."

"No, he doesn't."

The police and FBI looked as if they were packing their equipment to leave. It was too dark to see much of anything. Chief Murray walked over to the porch.

"Mr. Willard, we're about ready to head in for the night. We'll be back in the morning to have another look around for evidence."

And a look around for Regina, Jesse guessed.

"Chief, Mr. Willard just mentioned Dylan Morris used to work for him, and they had some problems."

Chief Murray's face betrayed no emotion. "That's interesting. I'll make a note of it. Do you need a ride home, Annabel?"

Annabel nodded toward her car. "Broken windows, but it's drivable. I'll finish up here and drive back to Granite Gulch."

"We've collected the bullets from the car, but bring it to work tomorrow. The FBI may want to look at it again."

They said their goodbyes. Chief Murray left in his police car. A few squad cars were parked in his driveway, presumably finishing their jobs.

Jesse was alone with Annabel, and while he should have been afraid of what the dark was hiding, he didn't feel fear. He liked being with Annabel.

"I have a hand vacuum we can use to clean out your car," he said.

"That would be nice. Thanks. Bummer that I'll need repairs," Annabel said. She shrugged. "It could have been worse. We could be in the hospital now."

After they removed the broken glass from her car, Jesse brought the vacuum inside. Annabel followed him, closing the front door behind her.

He noticed the coffee stains on her pants. "I should have offered earlier, but can I loan you a pair of pants?"

Annabel looked down at her jeans. "They're uncomfortable. Sticky. I might have put too much sugar in the coffee, trying to prove I'm a sweet person."

He grinned. "I have something that might fit you."

Jogging up the stairs to his room, he grabbed a pair of sweatpants with a drawstring waistband. He brought them to her and extended his hand. "Bathroom is around the corner."

Annabel thanked him and walked to the bathroom to change. Low maintenance woman. He liked women who were down-to-earth and practical. It fit with farm life. High-drama divas did nothing for him.

His thoughts switched to Annabel slipping into his pants. It had been a long time since a woman had undressed in his place. Not since he'd bought the farmhouse. He'd dated a few women and had spent time at their places, but he was too busy with work and his house-repair projects to be involved in a serious relationship. Picturing the other women he'd dated, he couldn't imagine them embracing farm life.

He could see Annabel at ease on the farm.

Annabel came around the corner, and she took his breath away. She was incredibly sexy with his pants slung on her hips. Maybe that's what did it for him. He had no right or reason to start drumming up lust-filled thoughts of the policewoman, but even knowing her job, knowing she suspected Regina, it didn't smother his desire completely.

He would have to be blind to miss that Annabel was sexy and beautiful and smart. What man didn't want that in his life? She had her folded pants in her hand.

He checked the floor for additional shards of glass,

realizing he had been staring at her with his mouth hanging open. At least he hadn't panted like a dog.

"Do you have a potato or a piece of bread?" she asked.

"Hungry?" He didn't know what food was in his pantry or refrigerator, but he had fresh produce at his fingertips.

She smiled. "Not hungry. I wanted to check for tiny bits of glass. I would hate for your dogs or cat to get a piece stuck in their paw."

Her consideration touched him. He found a loaf of bread, slightly stale, and they patted the area. When they were satisfied no glass remained, Annabel looked at him as if she had something to say.

"Speak your mind," he said. She had been forthcoming every other time they'd conversed. Why hold back now?

"I wanted to say I'm sorry again for my earlier questions. But this shooting could be connected to the Alphabet Killer."

It had crossed his mind, but only in the sense that the Alphabet Killer might have been targeting a new victim. "How do you figure?"

"The entire town knows your sister is a suspect. There's been a great deal of panicking about the Alphabet Killer. Then there's a shooting here."

She was looking for a lead. "Could be unrelated."

"Regina wrote in her letters to Matthew Colton that she understood harboring anger for a sibling."

Guilt slammed into him over the past. He'd heard rumors that Regina had been in touch with Matthew

Colton, but he'd ignored them, thinking no one in their right mind would willingly talk to the serial killer. Hearing Regina had written to Matthew Colton about him, even if she didn't mention him by name, was disturbing. "I don't blame Regina if she's angry at me. I expect it. When my mother left our father, she took me, but she didn't have custody of Regina. We left her alone with our father, and our father was not a nice man."

He could see Annabel wanted to ask him more. She might be a police officer, but she had questions like a detective. "You can't blame yourself for the decisions your mother made. I used to think I must have done something to make Matthew Colton unhappy at home. I tried to connect my actions as a child to his actions as an adult. They aren't related. Whatever you did when you were a boy and however that affects Regina, that's hers to deal with."

He liked what she was saying. Logically, he understood that he couldn't have done anything different to help Regina, but emotionally, it was hard to let go of the past. "Thanks for saying that." It unburdened his soul, though not entirely. Nothing could fully absolve him of the guilt he carried.

"Sure." She tossed the bread she'd been using in the trash and then walked slowly to the front door, grabbing her coffee-stained pants. She spun on her toes to face him. "I still owe you a cup of coffee."

He had long forgiven her, but he wouldn't turn down the opportunity to see her again. "Maybe next time I'm in town, I'll stop by the precinct and see if you're available."

"I'd like that."

He crossed to the door. He had manners; he would open it for her. Annabel was living up to that first impression he'd had of her. She was gorgeous, obviously, but she was thoughtful and classy and smart. How was this woman not already taken? Maybe she was as messed up as he was in relationships. Devastating childhoods left their mark, and that mark was often ugly and deep.

Their hands brushed, and electricity snapped between them. The air around them heated and sparked. She backed up against the door, her mouth tipped up invitingly. He set his hand on her chin, lightly, testing her reaction. He was aching to kiss her, and his palms itched to touch her. Did she want this, too?

They were coming off an adrenaline rush. Emotions and tensions were high. Even the mention of their childhoods was enough to stir their feelings. Were they looking to blow off steam or ignite something between them? They had chemistry. Being attracted to someone was easy, but having something mutual and hot and exciting was taking possibilities to the next level.

His body hardened, and he ached to pull her against him. The slightest touch, the briefest moment of friction, and it would feel so good.

Jesse brought his mouth closer to hers, maintaining eye contact. He was waiting for her to stop him.

And he would stop if she didn't want this. It might kill him, but he respected her and her boundaries.

Before their lips met, she turned toward the door, and he took a step back, feeling a chill rush between them.

"This isn't a good idea," she said.

If she was waiting for an agreement, she would be waiting for a long time.

"I need to go," she said.

She fled the house, and he stepped onto the porch, watching her leave. She slid into the driver's seat of her car. There were still two police cars in his driveway. Had they been waiting for Annabel?

As her car pulled away, she hit the brakes several times, but she didn't turn around.

When Annabel pulled up to her house, Trevor was there.

He climbed out of his car and waited on the sidewalk. Her body felt achy and grimy, and she wanted a hot shower, a bowl of soup and her bed. Being overly friendly now was beyond her. Trevor would understand that.

She walked past him. "We can talk tomorrow." She didn't want a lecture about Jesse. She didn't want to discuss the shooting or the Alphabet Killer.

"Annabel."

Couldn't he take a hint? Trevor was intuitive. The bigger issue was that he was bent on finding the Alphabet Killer, and nothing would stop him. She wanted Regina Willard found, too, but Annabel had hit her limit for the day.

Annabel almost ignored him and powered into the house and straight for her shower. She didn't need a critique of what she had done wrong at the scene. She had followed protocol, and she had protected herself and Jesse. That counted for something.

She turned. "It's been a long day, Trevor. I want to take a shower, eat a crappy canned dinner and go to sleep."

"Don't get defensive. I wanted to tell you that you did a nice job today. You handled yourself well."

She jolted at the compliment. "But…" There had to be more.

"No buts. You should know you're doing a good job."

Annabel felt emotion rising in her chest. It was sometimes hard for her to hug her brothers. She felt an invisible barrier between them, each of them allowing others in to a point, but she couldn't breach those depths. Familiarity had been lost when they'd been split up, and in her foster homes, affection was rare.

Figuring she had nothing to lose, she hugged Trevor quickly. "Thank you for saying that. It means a lot to me."

Trevor appeared uncomfortable. He shifted on his feet, running a hand through his dark hair. "You know we think you're a hard worker."

Annabel stared at him. "We? If you're referring to our brothers, I do not know what you all think, because you don't tell me. I sometimes think because I'm not in the boys' club, I miss the important stuff."

Trevor sighed. "It's late. We can talk about this later."

Figured. Anytime she broached emotional subjects with her brothers, she hit a wall with them.

"I wanted to be sure you got home okay," Trevor said.

In case she had decided to stay at Jesse's? What would he have done if she had? "I'm fine. 'Night, Trevor."

As she walked toward her porch, she saw a package. It wasn't the standard package from her favorite online retailer, and she wasn't expecting any other deliveries.

"Trevor?"

He was almost to the car, but he turned. "Yeah?"

"There's a package on my doorstep, and it looks weird."

Trevor was at her side in moments, his hand on his gun. Likely an instinct, since shooting the package would yield zilch.

"Could be nothing," she said, walking toward the door and not believing her words. Her arrest of Dylan Morris, the murder scene and the shooting at Willard's Farm had her feeling paranoid, as if there were a lot of bad things happening in Granite Gulch.

Trevor was on her heels as she moved closer. Her motion-sensor porch light snapped on, and the box burst into flames. Before she could register what was happening, Trevor was dragging her away from the house. A loud boom sounded and a shock wave knocked Annabel face-first into her front yard.

Her vision was blurry, and her ears were ringing. She rolled to her side to see the front of her house consumed in flames. Turning to see if Trevor was okay, she saw he was already on his phone.

Annabel didn't know how long she sat in front of her house, watching it burn, thinking about what she was losing inside her home. Her pictures, mementos from her life, from her foster mother Jean, from her mother, would be destroyed. Her life had been torn down by incidents in the past, and every time she had to rebuild, it had taken its toll on her.

Who had done this and why? Was this about the serial killings? A message from her father? He could have his admirers wreaking havoc at his command. Reasons as to why escaped her. Mostly, she felt the urge to cry. Her home was being consumed in flames.

A fire engine roared up her street, and Annabel rose to her feet. She needed to move out of the way to allow them through.

Standing on the sidewalk, her ears kept ringing. Trevor was speaking to her, but she couldn't understand him. Her house had been targeted by an arsonist and likely someone who wanted her dead.

As Jesse drove onto Main Street in Granite Gulch, he reassured himself that Annabel was fine. He'd been sitting on the porch with his dogs, waiting for the police to leave his property for the night and overheard a call over the radio. An incident had occurred at Annabel Colton's house, and Jesse wouldn't sleep without knowing if she was safe. He had caught the address over the radio, too.

His mind was buzzing with unanswered questions. Annabel believed the shooting was related to Regina, but additional trouble had followed Annabel home, meaning the shooter could be targeting her. Cops had a way of making enemies out of criminals.

Jesse had tried to call Annabel at the precinct, but she wasn't in and any message he left wouldn't get to her until her next shift.

With her protective brothers, Annabel was probably fine. Plus, she had proven to be brave and fierce. Those reminders didn't stop his worry.

Jesse drove closer to Annabel's house, and his uneasiness tripled. He smelled smoke, heard sirens and when he turned onto her street, worry morphed into panic. Police cars, fire trucks and ambulances filled the road.

He parked and climbed out of the car. Jogging down the street, relief passed over him when he saw Annabel standing on the sidewalk.

She was breathing. She was alive. She was staring at a house that was being doused by fire hoses spraying water.

He arrived at her side. "Annabel, is this your house? Are you okay?"

She turned to him, her eyes wide with fear and confusion. Her normally tidy ponytail was askew, and pieces had fallen out and were framing her face. It made her more lovely, although now wasn't the time to mention that. "Jesse," she said, her voice filled with surprise.

"I heard you had trouble tonight," he said.

"Word spreads like lightning in this town," she said. She was still wearing his pants.

"Are you all right? What happened?"

"Someone left a bomb in front of my door. It may have been motion- or light-activated, because it exploded when I was on the porch."

"You could have been seriously injured," Jesse said. Or killed, but he left those words unspoken.

Annabel's face was solemn. "I know. My brother was with me, too. He's okay, but this is bad."

Jesse was even more convinced this latest act of aggression had nothing to do with Regina. Annabel was incidentally involved in the Alphabet Killer cases like most officers of the Granite Gulch Police Department were, but Jesse wondered if the Alphabet Killer would target a police officer who wasn't directly involved in the case. "I'm sorry, Annabel. I can't imagine how you must feel." The fire seemed to be extinguished, but water continued to pour onto the house.

"You drove all the way from your farm to check on me?" Annabel asked, inclining her head.

"I don't have your phone number, and I was worried," he said.

She extended her hand. "Give me your phone, and we'll correct that. It will save you money in gas."

He didn't care about the expense or the time. He had needed to see her. He didn't want to look too deeply into that thought. She was a police officer who had accused Regina of being a serial killer. In addition to that, he had his own problems and time shortages. He wasn't interested in being involved with anyone anytime soon.

She handed him back his phone. "My partner and I arrested someone for assault and possession recently. He has the best lawyer in town because he was released on his own recognizance. I think he was letting me know that testifying against him would be a mistake."

"Did he leave your partner a threatening message, as well?" Jesse asked.

Annabel's eyes went wide. "I haven't heard anything, but I need to check in with Luis. Excuse me, just a minute." She took a few steps away to make her call.

Jesse watched the scene, looking for anyone who seemed out of place. The fire had drawn curious neighbors, some standing on their porches across the street, others on their lawns. The late hour wasn't keeping them inside. Other than having two serial killers in the past two decades, Granite Gulch wasn't a huge crime town, and everything that happened was still everyone's business.

Annabel returned to Jesse. "My partner is fine. His wife was angry that I woke him, but he checked his house and saw no sign of a package. This was about me. Maybe it wasn't about the arrest."

At least she hadn't suggested the arsonist was Regina.

Annabel bit her lip in worry. "Everyone is looking

for this guy. He won't get far. After he was arrested, blood tests confirmed he'd been high recently."

A previous conversation they'd had sprang to mind. "Dylan Morris? Did he do this?" Jesse asked.

"I shouldn't say anything until the investigation is complete," Annabel said.

Jesse didn't like what she wasn't saying. If he saw Dylan around, he would lay down the law with him, make it clear that if Dylan messed with Annabel, Jesse would make life harder for him. When Dylan was let go from the farm, Jesse had warned him not to use Jesse as a reference, but Jesse had not spread the word to other farmers and ranchers that Dylan was trouble.

Jesse believed in second chances, but he didn't believe in unlimited free range. Threating a woman crossed a line.

"Do you think the shooting this afternoon at my farm is connected to the fire?" Jesse asked.

Annabel twisted her lips in thought. Her kissable lips. "A shooting is aggressive. Leaving a bomb in a box on my doorstep is cowardly."

Jesse thought both were hostile actions. "To go to a police officer's house and set up a bomb is pretty bold. He knows where you live. He risked someone seeing him."

"The police are already canvasing the street, asking if anyone saw something unusual. Of course, in the most gossipy town in Texas, I'll bet no one has a solid lead."

"Does it bother you that he was close to your house?"

She shrugged. "Everyone knows where I live. This town is too small not to be aware of it or to figure it out by asking a few questions at the right places."

"What are you doing here?" The question from behind him was filled with anger and hostility.

Jesse turned and met the accusing stare of Sam Colton. Not that tonight was any reason to clink glasses together, but it seemed Sam was never smiling. He looked serious and resolute.

Annabel stepped between them. "Jesse was nice enough to check on me."

Sam narrowed his eyes. "It's late, Annabel. Are you staying with me or Trevor? I've already called Ridge, Ethan and Chris. You can stay with them, too."

The Coltons must like dragging each other into their problems. Nice that Annabel had options, and if Sam hadn't been standing right there, glaring at Jesse, Jesse would have offered Annabel his guest room. It was the gentlemanly thing to do.

"That's nice of you to offer," she said, "but I'll be staying with Mia."

Before Sam could protest, Annabel held up her hand. "I'll be fine at Mia's. Staying with her will be easier. I won't get on her nerves, and I don't relish the idea of sharing a bathroom or clothes with one of you."

Sam slid his hands into his pockets. "If that's what you want."

"That's what I want," Annabel said.

Jesse liked her independent streak. She didn't wait for someone to ride to her rescue. She made her own decisions.

Sam looked at Jesse again. "Are you planning to stick around?"

Annabel wasn't a piece of property they were fighting over, and Jesse wasn't interested in making an enemy of the Colton detective. "I'm heading home soon. I need to get up early tomorrow," Jesse said. As he did every day.

Jesse didn't like the Colton brother interfering in his private conversation with Annabel, but he understood the instinct to protect a sibling. What annoyed him was that the Coltons' dislike of him had more to do with his being Regina's brother than anything else.

Sam Colton took a few steps away.

Annabel touched Jesse's upper arm. "I'm sorry about that. It doesn't help his protective instincts that someone threatened me tonight."

"More than a threat. The front of your house was blown off," Jesse said.

Annabel looked at her house. Her shoulders sagged. He hadn't meant to put too fine a point on it, but he didn't want her in denial. This was a serious matter, and she had to be careful. If someone wanted her dead, they might not stop at a shooting and a bombing. Jesse wasn't familiar with the criminal psyche, but he guessed as bad as it seemed, this situation could escalate.

"I've called the insurance company. We'll have to sort it out in the morning. But when I find the person who did this to me, they'll know they messed with the wrong woman," Annabel said.

"Are you sure it wouldn't be easier to stay with one of your brothers? Or with me?" He wanted her to stay with someone who owned a gun and wasn't afraid to use it. Jesse didn't know her friend Mia well enough to know if she was armed and trained to use a gun.

Annabel jolted a bit. "Stay with you?"

He had crossed a line, and their near kiss snapped to mind. "In my guest room. We've protected ourselves from a shooter once and made a great team."

Annabel shook her head. "I'll be fine at Mia's. But your offer is tempting."

She said nothing else on the matter, but the look she gave him scorched him to the core. Was she acknowledging the heat between them, too?

"At least let me follow you to Mia's, so I know you're okay," Jesse said.

Annabel nodded. "Sure."

She climbed in her car and he into his. They made the short drive to her friend's house. She parked her car, and he stopped, planning to make sure she got into the house without a problem. Granite Gulch had been more violent than Jesse remembered it. The shooter from the ranch and the arsonist wouldn't likely stake out Mia's house, even if he was targeting Annabel. Given what Jesse had seen of Annabel's house, it was reasonable to assume the bomb had killed her.

Annabel walked to his truck, and he wound down the window of the car.

"I wanted to thank you for driving all this way to check on me," Annabel said.

"You're welcome. I'm being a gentleman."

Annabel smirked. "As long as you know that I may not always want you to be a gentleman. I like a man who's rough around the edges." She leaned forward and kissed his cheek before whirling away and jogging up to Mia's front door.

Jesse's response couldn't keep pace with his lust. There was an undercurrent of desire in her words. It wasn't just him who felt it. She had her reasons for keeping her distance, but she wasn't immune to his charms.

After she closed the door behind her, Jesse made the long drive to his farm, Annabel on his mind.

Chapter 7

Annabel had spent a frustrating morning on the phone with her home insurance company and was relieved when Sam asked her to meet him at the Java Hut.

He had a cup of her favorite coffee waiting.

"How are you holding up?" Sam asked.

"I feel weird wearing Mia's clothes. Didn't sleep well. But I suppose that's the least of my problems," Annabel said.

"Once the fire department clears the house, we'll help you search for anything salvageable," Sam said.

She appreciated that. She had plans to acquire some new clothes and personal items but hadn't had time yet. "I had a difficult morning on the phone with the insurance company. Let's talk about something else." The list of things to take care of with her house seemed endless. Stacking that on top of Dylan Morris's in-the-wind status and Annabel's few hours of sleep, she was cranky and overwhelmed.

Sam rolled his coffee cup between his hands. "The reason I asked you to meet me is that I'm worried you're hanging out with Jesse Willard."

"I'm not hanging out with Jesse Willard," Annabel said, trying to keep her cool. Her patience was frayed and her brothers could rile her frustration quickly.

"You two seemed friendly last night."

She didn't owe Sam an explanation, but she didn't want him making it his personal mission to dig around about her and Jesse. "I've been watching at his farm for his sister. No sign of her. I'm convinced he is not hiding her."

"A few hours watching his house can't make you sure of that."

Sam was impossible. "It's not watching his house that makes me sure. It's him. He doesn't know where she is. He isn't lying about that."

"I agree," Sam said.

That he didn't argue was a blessing.

"Jesse was genuinely worried about you. He wouldn't have driven to Granite Gulch to check on you if he was faking that emotion. Plus, we know his whereabouts for the afternoon. He didn't put that box on your doorstep."

"Then why are you objecting to us being friendly?" she asked. She didn't want to assign a word to their relationship, if she could call it that. A few chance meetings and nice conversations didn't amount to much. Even thinking it, she was lying to herself. She liked Jesse Willard more than she should.

"His sister is a killer," Sam said.

"He doesn't believe that, and our father is a killer. Does that mean I should warn Zoe to stay away from you?"

Sam frowned. "Of course not. Not that she would listen. But what we experienced with dad was twenty years ago. Jesse is facing these problems with his sister now."

"All the better he has people around who understand what he's going through."

"Are you trying to aggravate me? I'm worried about you, Annabel. Why do you have to make everything difficult? Why can't you stay away from him while this investigation is ongoing?"

Annabel laid her hand over her brother's. "I appreciate your concern. But I am fine. I know what I'm doing. I might be a rookie cop, but I'm still your older sister. I have years of life experience on you. If I'm assigned a stakeout at Willard's Farm, I'll take it and do my job. But I'll stay friendly with Jesse because we want him on our side. If he hears from Regina, I want him to tell us." Not just for that reason, but Jesse's connection to Regina was something Sam would be on board with.

"As long as you remember where the line is. I've been through this myself," Sam said. "Zoe was Celia's sister. It was weird for me and should have been a reason to stay away from her. I couldn't."

"And I'm glad for you. You've never been happier," Annabel said.

A dreamy look passed across Sam's face. He was thinking about Zoe.

He snapped back from his reverie quickly, saving Annabel from interrupting his Zoe daydream.

"Are you planning to take the day off? Chief said it was fine if you need a day to collect yourself," Sam said.

Annabel considered reporting for work, but she didn't have the energy and more phone calls awaited her. "I'll spend the day sorting what's left of my worldly possessions. Thank the chief for me."

She and Sam finished their coffees, keeping the conversation on topics other than murders, fires and serial killers.

When Sam left the Java Hut, Annabel stayed for a few extra minutes. Being in a crowd felt good. Though she wouldn't alarm her brothers by admitting she was rattled, she believed Dylan Morris had set the bomb, and he could be looking for her. The entire police force in Granite Gulch and neighboring counties were searching for Dylan, but with the Alphabet Killer at large, they were stretched thin as it was.

Would Dylan Morris try to kill her again? He could figure out where she was staying. He could watch her family and friends. Luis knew to be careful, but Dylan could catch him off guard. Nothing in Dylan's rap sheet indicated he had a preference for bomb making, but the internet was a treasure trove for those seeking to do harm.

Annabel's phone rang. Not recognizing the number, she answered, "Colton."

It was the fire chief, letting her know she could return to her house to collect anything that might have survived the fire. She figured she may as well, given her house was open, and eventually someone else would get the brilliant idea to search her things. She had little of value, but people could be nosy and rude.

"A structural engineer will be sent out to check the house and assess the damage. I'm sure you've been in touch with your insurance company?" the fire chief asked.

"Of course." Though they had been no help and borderline rude. She expected more from a company accustomed to dealing with customers who were facing difficult circumstances. She would have been happy if they had been compassionate, instead of asking questions that sounded like they were trying to wriggle out of approving the claim.

Annabel drove to her house. The sight in the light of day was no better. Someone had laid plywood sheets leading up to what was left of the front of the house. No front door. No porch swing. Her windows had been destroyed.

As she entered the house, she heard a creak from the back of the dwelling. Her gun safe was in the hall closet. The door was destroyed, but the safe was fireproof. She opened the closet and knelt on the floor. The outside of the safe was charred, but the combination worked. The lock popped, and Annabel lifted the lid and removed her gun.

Though her house didn't have a basement, the fire had damaged the structure, and she was unsure about the safety of the floors. She walked through the house, ignoring the debris and charred remains of her life.

Was someone already in her house? The fire chief had mentioned a structural engineer would take a look, but that would be a fast response time. Was it Dylan Morris? Regina Willard?

She turned the corner into the kitchen and lifted her gun. "Police, don't move." She came face-to-face with Jesse.

He was holding a piece of plywood in his hands. "Whoa, it's me. It's okay. I'm not looting."

She lowered her gun. "What are you doing here?"

"I've been doing construction on my farm. I had some leftover wood. I thought I would nail up your windows and maybe do something with the front of the house to protect it from the weather."

Annabel blinked at him. "You don't have to do that."

His face flickered with an emotion she couldn't read.

She was acting ungrateful and she needed friends. "You're kind to help me."

The electricity had been turned off after the incident and, therefore, no air-conditioning. A small sheen of sweat covered Jesse's face. What was it about a working man that was incredibly sexy?

"Just being friendly," Jesse said.

The same word she'd used to describe their relationship to Sam. Jesse was circling her as much as she was circling him. After the near kiss the night before at his place, she couldn't blame him. She didn't know where she stood with Jesse, and she was afraid to ask him.

Annabel assisted him with the wood. "They may tear down the house." The idea saddened and angered her, a potent mix that made her feel dizzy. She had worked hard to buy this house, and it was her home, the first place where she had felt secure. She had believed no one could make her leave. But apparently, a bomb could force her out. Why was it so hard to find anything stable and reliable in her life?

The emotion, the heat and Jesse were close to making her swoon. And Annabel wasn't a woman who swooned.

"Think positive. It could be repaired," Jesse said.

"How did you get handy around the house?" Annabel asked, not wanting to give in to the emotion. Crying wouldn't help anything, and it would make her feel worse.

"Learned from doing miscellaneous jobs. I was the man of the house from a young age, and my mom didn't have money to pay contractors to fix broken stuff. I did the best I could to help her."

Though she rarely thought about the house she had grown up in, her thoughts turned to the ramshackle farmhouse on the outskirts of town. She had good memories of the house and of the big country kitchen, where the family had spent their time when they were indoors. Many days they were outside, running free. They'd owned five acres, none of it used for farmland, and even though Matthew worked as a handyman, Annabel remembered something was always broken.

Without any maintenance or care, the house was a mess now. Peeling white clapboard, and Annabel imagined the inside was wrecked by the weather, neglect and vandals. On the rare occasions that Annabel drove past the house, she could hardly believe it was the house where she'd lived. It was run-down, and the land looked dry and barren. She didn't know who owned it. She guessed the state, and no one wanted to buy the house where the gruesome murder of Saralee Colton had taken place.

At least, that was what Ethan had reported: that their mother had been lying on the floor of the living room, bleeding, and with red circles drawn on her forehead. Ethan didn't speak of that day often. Though Annabel couldn't imagine their mother leaving them, she had hoped and wished Ethan had been mistaken, and their mother had run away.

"Hey, are you all right?" Jesse asked, taking her arm.

Annabel snapped to focus. "I'm fine. My mind was wandering."

"To what?" Jesse asked.

"The house where I grew up."

"What about it?"

"It looks different now than I remember. I haven't been inside the house in years, and I don't have any intention of visiting, but it haunts me. I wish the state would tear it down and build something in its place. Maybe a housing development or a shopping center, something to scrub that place off the face of the earth."

She hadn't meant to sound bitter, but their mother hadn't been found, and it was a source of great pain.

Matthew had scared her as a child, and when she thought of him, she saw his picture in the newspapers from twenty years ago. He had seemed disturbed and crazy.

"Maybe someone will do that," Jesse said. "I know the place you're talking about, and it's decent land. It could be used for something positive for the town."

Annabel was keen on the idea. Much like her and her brothers working to be good people, the house could be good for someone, too. "My sister and I used to stay up late and talk. When my father was ranting and raving, I would climb into bed with Josie and cuddle her close. It made us both feel better. Now, my sister won't talk to me."

"Why won't she speak to you? Too much for her to cope with?" Jesse asked.

Since Jesse had experience dealing with a difficult sister, Annabel felt comfortable confiding in him. "She hasn't said why she's angry at us."

"Maybe she's not angry. Maybe she's handling the situation the best she can, and seeing you is too hard. It reminds her of good times or bad times or whatever is most troubling to her," Jesse said.

Annabel had considered that, and though it was difficult for her to imagine Josie was angry about something her siblings had done—or hadn't done—twenty years before, Annabel still felt guilty.

She would call or visit Josie if she knew where she was or had any leads to find her. She wanted her sister to have the opportunity to speak her mind, maybe get something off her chest she may have been carrying around for two decades.

"If Josie would communicate, even in an email or a phone call, we could help her. We can relate to how she feels. We're in the same boat with our parents and living with what Matthew Colton did to us."

"That's how I feel about Regina, that if she would talk to me about our father, I could help her," Jesse said.

Annabel cringed. The Alphabet Killer investigation had firmly shifted from Josie as a suspect to Regina Willard.

"I sometimes think Josie could have gotten tied up in drugs or alcohol." She could be suffering from the same mental disease that had made their father kill innocent people. Whatever was preventing Josie from coming home, it couldn't be unforgivable or unfixable. Even if Josie had followed in her father's footsteps, at least they could get Josie the help she needed.

"I think people with childhoods like the ones we had often self-medicate. But you have to do what I do with Regina. I know she'll come around eventually, and when she does, I'll be open and ready to talk."

It was how Annabel felt about Josie. No matter when or where, Annabel wanted her sister in her life.

* * *

Annabel arrived at work twenty minutes late. Given the past couple of days and what she had been through, she didn't expect anyone to comment on her tardiness.

Sam was speaking to Chief Murray, who looked up when she entered the precinct. Her heart dropped. Maybe he was angry she was late. He had given her a day off to deal with her problems, which was more than the department could spare. Maybe she had done something else wrong.

The chief motioned for her to come to his office. Keeping her head held high, Annabel strode to the office and entered.

"Glad to see you in one piece this morning," Chief Murray said.

"No further incidents," Annabel said, trying to appear casual. Though she was comfortable at Mia's place, Annabel hadn't slept well, tossing and turning and worrying about Josie, the Alphabet Killer, her house and her brothers. Thinking of Jesse had stolen some sleep from her as well, her body charged with erotic energy and having no outlet for it.

"We don't have the identity of the shooter from Willard's Farm, and we haven't received confirmation the bomb left at your house was made by Dylan Morris. I have everyone on patrol looking for him. Until we have more leads, I want you on modified assignment."

That meant endless hours at the information desk. She had earned her first shift not at a desk and not walking the streets of Granite Gulch, handing out tickets and taking the most boring calls. She wouldn't be shoved back into the land of tedium now.

"Will Luis be on modified assignment, as well?" Annabel asked.

The chief folded his hands on his desk. "No. He was not shot at, and his house was not bombed."

Good point, except Luis had as much to worry about from Dylan Morris as she did. Annabel hated sitting at a desk. It didn't suit her. And while she would do her shifts at the mundane yet essential tasks, she had taken more than her fair share of rotations on the information desk. "With all due respect, is this request coming from my brother?"

Annabel wouldn't look at Sam. If she did, she wouldn't be able to control her temper. If he wanted her on modified assignment, he should have told her at the café yesterday. Sam was a hotshot police detective, the youngest the precinct had ever had, and his ego made him think he could decide what the entire police force in Granite Gulch did and where they went. His instincts were often spot-on, but in this case, Annabel could keep herself safe.

Chief Murray took a sip of his coffee. "Detective Colton mentioned it may be safer for you. The safety of my officers is my primary concern."

Though Annabel had been trained to respect the chain of command, she wanted to be treated fairly. If she wasn't Sam's sister, she wouldn't be put on the bench. "Sir, I don't think it's necessary for me to be placed on modified assignment. I handled myself per protocol in both the shooting at Willard's Farm and when the bomb was set at my house. I think that garners me credit. I've been useful to the department and not just when I'm answering phone calls. I made the connection between Regina Willard and Matthew Colton and the Rosewood Rooming House. I've handled my cases, even the small or seemingly insignificant ones, with professionalism and integrity."

The chief nodded. Was that respect in his eyes? "I'd make this suggestion to any of my officers who were dealing with a suspect where the case turns personal. You're safer behind a desk."

"I can handle it."

"Annabel, you're new. You don't know what could be waiting for you on the street. Dylan Morris could find you," Sam said.

He may have felt she needed to hear this, in case she was in denial about the bombing. "I realize what Dylan Morris can do. I will be careful. Would you accept desk duty under the same circumstances? How many criminals have you put behind bars? Do you know where they are now? Do you worry about them coming to hurt you?" Annabel asked.

"Every day, Annabel, I worry about Zoe and me," Sam said.

"You don't have to worry about me. I can handle myself, especially against a punk like Dylan Morris," Annabel said.

She and Sam locked eyes, and neither was willing to give.

The chief broke in, clearing his throat. "It's your

decision, Annabel. If you want to be on the street, then fine. If you change your mind, you know my door is open. No one will think less of you for taking the safe option," Chief Murray said.

Except Annabel would think less of herself. She couldn't remember another instance where a police officer had taken desk duty because they were involved with a difficult criminal.

Before Sam could protest or state his case again, Annabel smiled her thanks. "Thanks, Chief. I'll be careful."

Annabel hurried to check in with her sergeant. Her assignment for the day was handing out parking tickets along Main Street. The Spring Fling was coming up, and cars were double-parked and causing congestion. It wasn't the best assignment, but it was better than answering phones.

After getting another uniform to wear since hers had been burned to ash, Annabel and Luis parked along Main Street and started on foot. Handing out parking tickets would take an hour at most, and as long as they didn't get into an altercation with anyone, they'd be back on patrol soon after.

Annabel pulled her ticket book from the glove box and handed Luis his. They walked along the street, recording tickets for cars illegally parked. It made for a bad day for the people receiving the tickets, but it was her job to enforce the law, not worry about someone having a rough day.

"Annabel!" Luis called to her.

Annabel jogged to where Luis was standing next

to a light blue pickup, a rusty patch along the passenger side. The windows were grimy. A few faded bumper stickers were attached to the bed of the truck. Peering inside the cab, Annabel saw a gun sitting on the backseat, some empty vodka bottles on the floor and a baseball bat.

"Is this the truck that drove away from the assault next to the Bar and Saloon?" Luis asked.

Annabel hadn't been close enough to read the license plate. The rust spots were where she remembered and might be enough for probable cause. "We'll call for a warrant to be sure."

Annabel took pictures of the car while Luis called the station.

"Hey, get away from my car!" A man was running down the street toward them. Was he one of the men from the assault who had fled on foot?

Luis put away his phone, and Annabel held out her hands. "Sir, calm down. We have a few questions for you."

The man launched himself at Luis, who was closer. The two men slammed into the pickup. Luis wrestled for control and struck the man. The man stumbled back. Annabel moved closer to assist.

Luis seemed to be holding his own, but the faster they had the man in custody, the better. The man lunged at Luis, and Annabel saw the glint of metal in his hand.

"Luis, he has a knife!" Annabel shouted the warning as she dove at the man, trying to bend his arm away from Luis.

He was too strong, and Annabel's adrenaline kicked hard when Luis cried out in pain and threw the man off him. The attacker hit a mailbox and slumped onto the sidewalk. Annabel kicked his hand, knocking away the knife.

Before he could gather himself to strike again, she rolled the man facedown on the ground. She shoved her knee into his lower back and secured his hands with her cuffs, wrapping them around the mailbox. He could stay put until help arrived.

"If you wanted it rough, you could have just asked. Happy to oblige a pretty lady," the assailant said.

Idiot. As if she hadn't heard every innuendo related to sex and her cuffs already. He sounded drunk or high, and he was a fool to attack two uniformed police officers. "Shut up and stay on the ground unless you want a bullet in your head." She considered giving his head a thump against the sidewalk in case he had any ideas of trying to fight, but she decided Luis was more important.

Annabel called on her radio for backup and an ambulance and checked on Luis. He was bleeding from a wound on his side. He was pressing his hands over the area. Annabel removed her blue uniform shirt and set it on Luis's torso. He winced, but she needed to keep pressure on it. As the navy fabric grew darker with Luis's blood, Annabel felt an ominous wave pass over her. The attacker had struck hard and deep.

"You handled him well," Annabel said.

"He got me," Luis said. Luis was strong and a big guy, and few got the better of him in a fistfight.

"He's on something. Maybe amphetamines," Annabel said.

"What's happening to this town?" Luis said. He closed his eyes, and panic fluttered inside her stomach. Staying conscious was important.

"Your wife will be pretty pissed," Annabel said.

Luis snorted. "Let's not tell her about this."

From what Annabel had witnessed about Beatrice and Luis's relationship, Luis enjoyed it when his wife fussed over him. "I'll see what I can do."

The assailant was making comments, but Annabel ignored him. She was relieved when she heard sirens approaching. When the EMT and paramedics arrived on the scene, police backup was on their heels. Two other officers took the assailant into custody, and Annabel followed the ambulance to Blackthorn County General in her police cruiser.

Annabel had been waiting in the ER for three hours. Luis's wife and children had arrived about an hour after she had, and they were with him. He'd needed surgery to repair the damage from the stabbing, but the doctors expected a full recovery.

Luis's wife came into the ER from the patient room area, looking around and smiling when she saw Annabel. Annabel rose to her feet. Guilt assailed her. Her partner had been hurt while they were in the field. She should have done something to stop the attacker before he was close enough to harm anyone.

"Luis was hoping you'd stayed," Beatrice said.

"I wanted to make sure he was okay and you didn't

need anything," Annabel said. She had been running the event through her mind and looking for places where she could have responded differently and changed the outcome.

Beatrice hugged her. "He told me what you did. You saved his life. Thank you. I feel ridiculous saying that because it's not enough, but thank you. When Luis told me he'd been paired with the rookie, I was nervous. But Luis kept telling me how well you were doing and how hard you were working."

Luis had said that about her? Beatrice could have knocked her over with a feather. No one on the police force was quick to hand out compliments, especially to the rookie. Hearing Luis spoke well of her was almost as nice as if she had heard the comment directly.

"Thank you for saying that. This was the first time I've dealt with a situation like this. Luis has been a good teacher."

Beatrice squeezed her hand. "Would you mind talking to him for a minute? He's tired, and the medication will probably put him to sleep soon, but he wanted to speak with you."

Annabel nodded and hid her surprise. They hadn't been partners for long, and he resented her for the boring assignments in Granite Gulch being passed to them.

Annabel followed Beatrice to Luis's room. Beatrice excused herself, and Annabel was alone with Luis.

"Thank you for what you did today," Luis said. He

sounded tired and looked pale, but his monitors were beeping steadily, and his vitals were green.

"You're welcome. You'd have done the same for me," Annabel said.

"Guess this means you're not a rookie anymore," Luis said. "Murder scene, shoot-out and a stabbing."

"It's been a bad week," Annabel said.

Luis didn't usually speak to her this way, as if they were colleagues. It made her feel respected as his partner for the first time.

"Some weeks are like that. No matter what, we have to get back on the horse," he said.

She nodded. "You may need a couple days. Taking a knife to the side is a good reason to let someone else take the reins for a bit."

He laughed and then winced. "A couple days. Then I'll be back."

"Get some rest. I'll keep your saddle oiled."

She left the room. Beatrice was standing outside. "Thank you again, Annabel. When Luis is better, we'll have you over for dinner."

"I'd like that," Annabel said. Being invited for dinner was a gesture no one else on the force had made, except Sam, who'd had her over as family, not as a colleague.

As Annabel was walking through the ER on her way to the parking lot, a familiar face was standing at the discharge desk, signing papers.

Jesse Willard's right hand was wrapped in bandages. He was writing awkwardly with his left. Concerned, Annabel crossed to where he was standing. "Jesse? Everything okay?"

He smiled as he turned to her. He handed the papers to the administrator with a word of thanks. "Officer Colton. I'm fine. Minor incident with a broken tractor. Thought I could fix it alone and cut my hand."

"That's a big bandage for a minor incident," she said.

"Eight stitches, but I've had worse. What brings you here in uniform? Official police business?"

They walked toward the exit. "My partner and I had a run-in with a civilian today. Luis was stabbed."

Concern darkened Jesse's face, and his green eyes studied her. "Is he okay?"

"We were lucky. He'll recover." A wave of emotion passed over her, and she took a deep breath. "Sorry, it's hot in here."

"I'm sure you're overwhelmed. The adrenaline and the worry propels you, and when everything is fine, the emotion catches up. It's okay if you need to cry."

She wouldn't cry in uniform. She shook her head, trying to throw off the heavy emotion pressing on her. "I need to eat." She was suddenly craving a box of cookies and a handful of jelly beans. She wanted sugar when she was upset. When she remembered she couldn't go home, she wanted to add apple pie to her menu.

"You sure? If you need someone to listen, I'm happy to be a sounding board," Jesse said.

He was being nice to her. Again. How did he do that? If the tables were turned, she would be hostile, cagey and rude. Annabel didn't tolerate anyone speaking badly about her brothers or sister, even when they said things she knew were true.

She wanted to return some of the favor to Jesse for his kind offer. "Can I give you a ride?"

Jesse looked at his hand. "Actually, that would be great. Grace dropped me off. She had to pick up her son at school. My other option is an expensive taxi ride."

They walked through the parking lot of the hospital.

"You and Grace are close?" Annabel asked.

"She's great."

Jesse was talented at not answering questions. Was Grace his lover? His girlfriend? Before she could ask, he groaned. "The police cruiser? Talk about rumors spreading."

"You don't have to ride in the back. Sit up front with me. Maybe that will dispel rumors. Jesse Willard, friend to the police."

"I think your brothers would have something to say about that," Jesse said, climbing in the passenger side of the car.

Annabel opened her door and sat, starting the car. "What would they have to say about it?"

"They'd want to clarify that while I may be friendly to the police, my relationship with the police, especially one female Colton officer, does not extend into friendship or anything more."

When he said "anything more," her body heated. She turned up the air conditioner in the car. "If my brothers had their way, I wouldn't have anything more with a man during my lifetime."

"They see you as their little sister to protect," Jesse said.

That was about right. She was older than Sam, Ridge and Ethan, but they acted as if she was the child who needed guidance. "I don't know how much you know about my family. Most people know about Matthew Colton and what he did, the people he killed. While he was in police custody, my brothers and I were sent to separate foster homes. We rarely saw each other. I was only close with my twin brother because we were in the same school district and attended high school together."

"I'm sorry. I'm sure that's been difficult for you all."

She should change the subject, but it felt good to talk about this. Jesse didn't seem overly judgmental about Matthew Colton. To date, he'd had plenty of opportunities to make snide comments about her father, but he'd refrained. He also didn't gloss over what had happened to them, as if they'd deserved to be punished for their father's crimes. "It has been rough at times. When my oldest brother turned eighteen, he tried to gain custody of the rest of us." Though it hadn't happened immediately, Trevor had led the charge to reunite the family.

Conversation flowed between them, easy and open, despite the topic. It was refreshing to talk to Jesse. She could say almost anything to him.

Too soon and wishing they had more time, Annabel pulled up to Willard's Farm. The lights were on around the barn, but the house was dark. "Let me check the front door and make sure you don't have anyone waiting for you inside." The shooter was still at large, identity in question.

Jesse shot her a look. "I've been coming home without a police escort for years. I'll manage."

He climbed out of the car, and Annabel followed him to the porch. She didn't like the pitch-black, a hiding place for lurkers. Jesse opened his front door.

"You don't lock your door?" she asked.

Jesse rolled his shoulders. "No. Should I?"

"Given what's been happening around here, yes, you should."

Jesse turned on the lights and closed the door behind her, making a show of locking it. "If it makes you sleep better at night, I'll lock up."

"That's a start," she said.

He laughed, a deep chuckle, and it was impossible not to smile. "I'm antagonizing you. I usually lock the door when I'm out, but I left in a hurry and I didn't think about the door. I'll be more careful."

"Can I lend you a hand since yours is injured?" Annabel asked.

"Grace said she fed the dogs, but they'll be anxious to see me and eat again. Can you pour their food in their bowls?"

They walked to the kitchen. Annabel took the bag of dog food from the pantry and filled the yellow and blue bowls on the floor.

Jesse opened the back door and whistled. His dogs

came running. Not to be left out, Diva strode into the room, watching the dogs and Annabel. "I assume you're hungry, too?" Annabel asked.

She meowed.

"She's mad because her dinner is late. Her wet food is in the cans above the sink," Jesse said.

Annabel retrieved the cat food, gold-labeled, top-of-the-line stuff, and pulled off the lid of the can. She dumped the food into Diva's glittery pink bowl.

"Now that the most important members of the family are happy, we can eat. Dinner's beef stew from a can. Might be easier if you'd pop the can open. Open two if you'd like to join me. I'd enjoy the company."

Meals in a can weren't her top pick for dinner, but she was hungry, and beef stew was better than emotionally eating the contents of the cookie jar and candy tin at Mia's. "Where are your pots?"

He pointed, and she grabbed a pot from the location he indicated. It was a quality brand and, like the rest of his house, clean. "This is not what I would expect for a bachelor."

She popped the lids and peeled off the tops of the cans. She dumped the contents in the pot.

"I've been alone a long time. I had to acquire some basic kitchen skills and supplies for survival. But the truth is, if I were eating alone, I would have eaten the stew straight from the tin."

She wrinkled her nose. "Room temperature?"

He shrugged. "It gets the job done."

"Please tell me you eat better than frozen meals and meat from a can." Not that she had room to criticize. Her best cooking skill was pressing buttons on the microwave.

"Usually Grace has something ready for me for dinner."

Annabel had almost forgotten about the willowy brunette who moved like her name. Jesse mentioned her often enough to indicate they were close, and that had Annabel curious.

This wasn't a date, and envy had no place in this relationship. She decided to ask the question plain. "Is Grace your girlfriend?"

Jesse lifted his brow.

Annabel focused on looking for a spoon to stir the stew. "I'm an interested person. You mention her a lot. I wanted to know."

"Grace works for me. She's involved with someone else."

She caught something in his voice. "Does that upset you?" Was he jealous of Grace's boyfriend?

"It upsets me that she's involved with an idiot."

"You sound jealous," she said.

Jesse shook his head. "It's not like that with Grace and me. She's a great lady, and I wish her all the happiness in the world, but she has to stop hooking up with jobless losers who use her and jerks who don't treat her well. She's like a little sister. When this whole business with the Alphabet Killer started, I worried about Grace being targeted. I've been keeping her close and keeping her safe. She's a single mom to the coolest kid this side of the Mississippi."

His affection for her sounded sincere and decidedly nonsexual. "I've seen people I care about in terrible relationships. But I've also recently seen my three brothers with the right women, and it's inspiring. Maybe Grace will find someone worthy of her."

"What about you? Have you found someone?"

Annabel located two bowls in the cabinets to the left of the stove. She shut off the burner and poured some of the stew into each. Bringing it to the table, she set it down in front of Jesse. "I haven't and I won't. I've had too many bad experiences."

Jesse took two spoons from the drawer and set them on the table. "What can be so bad that you're off men completely?"

"Look at my father. That type of thing messes with me."

"We didn't have the best examples of a healthy relationship growing up. That does screw with you."

"It sure does." Annabel took a spoonful of stew. She didn't want to talk about her relationship failures. She hadn't had a decent, intimate relationship with a man. She chased men away. She was anxious she would pick a jerk and not see who he was until she was married to him. Annabel could pick a man who was deranged like her father and be chained to a monster.

Is that how her mother had felt about Matthew Colton?

Her mother had seen something good in Matthew. She wouldn't have stuck around for so long if she hadn't. Or maybe Saralee had felt trapped. She'd had seven children and few job skills. Her mother hadn't talked about how she had met Matthew or what she had seen in him. Her father was intelligent, and Annabel wondered if he had tricked her mother.

Annabel hadn't doubted her mother's love for her. Saralee had taken in sewing to put food on the table, bartering her needle-and-thread skills for food.

Jesse was eating slowly and seemed to be concentrating hard.

"Are you feeling okay?" Annabel asked.

Jesse blushed. "Eating with my left hand is a challenge, and I'm trying not to spill. Wiping food off my face and shirt like a nine-month-old isn't sexy. But don't offer to feed me, because I have some pride."

Annabel smiled. "Don't worry. This is Texas. I know a thing or two about a man's pride."

When they were finished eating, Annabel cleared away the dishes and washed them. Jesse needed to keep his bandages dry. "Is there anything else you need before I leave?"

Jesse shook his head. "Thanks for being good company tonight. It was nice having someone to eat with. I love my dogs and Diva, but they don't converse well."

Jesse escorted her to the front door. Annabel put her hand on the door handle and remembered the last time they were in this position. Jesse had almost kissed her, and she had turned away.

Now, he was watching her, but not looking as if he'd make a move. That was good, right? She couldn't have a personal relationship with a person of interest on this case, and she had made that clear. If there had been any doubt in his mind about the possibility of a future, however brief, her brothers had rammed it away. "Hope your hand is feeling better." She wished she had something more clever to say, but it was hard, when the only thoughts going through her mind had to do with kissing Jesse and running her hands over those ripped biceps and abdominals.

She looked at him, taking in his light hair, his piercing green eyes and his ruggedly handsome face. He was in need of a shave, but he looked good to her. Too good.

Their eyes met and held. Her heart hammered, and some invisible force beckoned to her. Her hands ached to touch him.

"Forget this. I might have a busted hand, but I'm still a man," Jesse said. He advanced on her and, using his left hand, lifted her mouth to his.

He brought his mouth down on hers possessively. Everything in the kiss was demanding and hungry. Her body responded to his touch, her desires rising and taking hold. She was starving for him. She kissed him in return, opening her mouth beneath his, reveling in the press of his firm lips to hers and shifting closer to him. She slid her foot between his, their thighs brushing, their hips connecting.

His tongue stroked hers, in an intensely erotic and pleasurable activity. She could have kissed Jesse Willard for hours.

He moved his left hand to her lower back, bracing his injured one on the door. The brush of their pants sparked friction in the right places. Arching her hips, she rolled them into Jesse.

Jesse broke the kiss, his forehead touching hers. "That was better than I had fantasized."

"In your fantasy, was I wearing my uniform? Because in my fantasies, you're in boots and spurs and a cowboy hat, but I'm the one who does the riding."

The words tumbled from her lips. She didn't usually speak explicitly, but he had flipped a switch in her brain and she was bent on the idea of more, fixated completely on her hormones and her racing heartbeat.

His eyes burned with lust. He'd liked what she'd had to say.

"When I ran into you that first day at the precinct, you were wearing your uniform. I thought about what you'd look like without it."

"Without it or without anything?" she asked.

"The second one," he said. His breath was coming in rapid, even puffs.

She was swept up in this moment, and her body ached, her lips felt raw.

As her pulse slowed and the blood rushed back to her head, she knew she shouldn't be in his house, kissing him. A person of interest was off-limits to an officer or detective working a case. She was not the lead detective, but she'd gone to the scene at Gwendolyn's house, and she had read the letters her father had received from Regina Willard and she had been assigned the stakeout at this farm.

Kissing the killer's brother hadn't been part of the plan.

Chapter 8

Despite his claims he was fully capable of returning to work, Luis was on medical leave until his doctors cleared him to work again. Chief Murray was open to putting Luis on administrative duty, but too much time filing paperwork and answering phones would make Luis feel worse. Luis needed to rest and heal. That was best accomplished under Beatrice's watchful eye and, from Luis's description, her amazing skills in the kitchen.

Without her partner available, Annabel was given temporary assignments, filling in for other officers who'd called in sick or helping at traffic accident scenes. She enjoyed the variety of the work. Every day was a new challenge. The search continued for Dylan Morris. The GGPD had tracked him to an apartment where he had been staying, but instead of Dylan, they had found a drug house, complete with ten pounds of heroin ready for sale and enough marijuana to get the entire town stoned. They had collected the evidence, and Chief Murray was pleased the drugs were off the street, but they still hadn't located Dylan.

When Chief Murray asked her to head back to Willard's Farm for another stakeout, Annabel had mixed emotions.

She thought about the kiss she had shared with Jesse, but she hadn't told anyone about it. No one, that is, except Mia. Mia had cheered her on, telling her she had to take the bull by the horns. Annabel hadn't been the aggressor in the relationship, and she kept throwing on the brakes. If she wanted anything to happen again, would she need to initiate it?

Annabel wasn't worried about her safety at Jesse's farm. Jesse was a good man, and he would look out for her. The stakeout was a waste of time. Jesse wasn't hiding Regina. Other officers had been placed on stakeout duty at Willard's Farm, and their reports were consistent with hers. Same employees arriving and leaving at regular times and no sign of Regina Willard. There had been no further criminal incidents at Willard's Farm since the shooting.

The chief clapped her on the shoulder. "Annabel, I know it seems like a waste, but until we have a better lead on Regina, we're watching Willard's Farm. I have officers checking in with the Rosewood Rooming House, too. I doubt Regina will return there or to any place where we know she's been, but we have to find her. We're accountable to the public, and every dark-haired woman whose name or nickname starts with *H* is terrified."

Annabel understood. She wouldn't argue with the chief. "Okay, sir. I understand. I'll head out to Jesse's, that is, Willard's Farm now." She cleared her throat.

The chief lifted his brow, but didn't comment on her slip of the tongue calling Jesse by his first name.

"Please, do. Report on my desk tomorrow, but call if you see anything of note," Chief Murray said.

After making the drive to Willard's Farm, Annabel chose a different location to watch. Though this stakeout wouldn't contribute to the case, she wouldn't make her actions predictable. If Regina was waiting for the right time to approach her brother, she was smart enough to wait until the police weren't actively watching the farm.

Annabel had been sitting in the vehicle, camera on the passenger seat, for close to forty-five minutes when she snagged a glimpse of Jesse. Her breath caught in her throat.

He was wearing jeans and boots, and the cuffs of his green plaid shirt were rolled to the elbows. He did a double take when he spotted the car and then started walking toward it. Annabel sat up straighter and smiled.

As Jesse neared the car, she read the look on his face. He was not pleased to see her.

"What brings you out to my farm this morning, Officer Colton?"

If she had been uncertain about his reaction to seeing her, his words confirmed it. He was being formal and cold, and she didn't like it. Jesse had to understand she didn't want to be on this stakeout, but she was finally getting actual police assignments and she didn't want to ruin it by complaining.

"Still looking for the Alphabet Killer," she said. "Luis is on leave. I've been working whatever assignments the chief sends my way." She wanted it to be clear she was not doing this to anger Jesse or because she believed he knew where Regina was hiding.

"Do you have a lead on the shooter from the other day?" he asked.

"A few questions we're chasing down answers to, but nothing solid." The ballistics on the bullets found at Jesse's farm and the bullet used in the Alphabet Killer murders were not from the same gun.

Regina might be using multiple weapons, but to date, they had tied the crimes by the bull's-eye signature at the scene and the letters in the victim's names. Regina could have broken her pattern to seek revenge against her brother. Annabel wasn't ruling her out.

"Have you found Dylan Morris?" Jesse tipped his hat back on his head.

"Not a whisper," she said.

"I have some friends keeping an eye out for him. He used to hang out at the same locations, and if he still has a drug problem, he's likely to surface at those places looking for a score."

Since learning about the drug house, Annabel was sure Dylan was a dealer and a user. "What places are those?" she asked. If Jesse had specifics, she would chase the leads.

Jesse folded his arms. "Can't say for sure. I've been asking around. I'm surprised he would shoot at us from any distance. From what I remember, he wasn't a good shot."

"Since he missed me, I would say that's still the case."

"He must be some fool, though. Who knowingly shoots at a police officer?"

Annabel nodded. "The arrest Luis and I made wasn't personal, but the bomb at my house was. If Dylan is responsible, and the evidence is pointing to him, he took this to the next level, and that wasn't wise. My brothers have it out for him. God help him if they find him first." She could see them wailing on Dylan before he had a chance to give his statement.

"Are you planning on sticking around long?" Jesse asked.

"For the rest of my shift," Annabel said.

Jesse nodded once as if he understood. Annabel knew he was angry.

"I know you don't know where Regina is. What if she shows up here?" Annabel asked. "I want to find Regina and speak with her, but I want to keep you safe, too."

"I've told you before. I have nothing to fear from Regina. She's my sister. She wouldn't hurt me or anyone else."

Denial was hard and strong in Jesse. "I'll be out here watching if anything happens."

Jesse sighed. "I'm sorry this case is putting us on opposite sides. I had hoped we'd find common ground and make nice."

"I'd like that, too." They had found common ground in their attraction to each other. Was it enough? Would it last until the Alphabet Killer was apprehended?

Jesse rolled his shoulders. "I don't know what's going on with us, but you're a cop and I'm related to a person wanted by the police and FBI. That seems complicated."

"It doesn't have to be complicated. No one is perfect, and nothing is without flaws. I'm related to a criminal, and I'm a cop," she said. She understood Jesse was a loyal brother and a good citizen. In this case, he couldn't be both. "It can work."

"I don't know how it will work, but at least I'm in good company in my confusion. I don't think either of us knows what we want right now."

That wasn't entirely true. Annabel wanted Jesse, but she wasn't brave enough to speak the words.

Grace was waiting in the kitchen when Jesse entered. He was in a foul mood. The irrigation equipment in one of his cotton fields was going haywire, turning on too often at times and not turning on when it was needed. Annabel had resumed her post near his property. He had half a mind to invite her on to the farm and let her poke around, but he was running a business, and he wouldn't open that door to the GGPD. Sooner or later, they would realize they were wasting their time and resources watching Willard's Farm and leave him alone.

"Jesse, I need to talk to you."

Grace had her arms folded over her chest, and she was tapping her toe.

"What's on your mind?" he asked, sitting down and trying not to let his annoyance with his problems reflect in his voice.

"I told you that I was pregnant. I was living with my boyfriend." Her voice cracked, and she broke down into tears. "But he kicked me out. Noah and I have no place to go. We're staying with my sister for a few days, but she doesn't want us around. We're crowding her."

Jesse's chest tightened. "I'm sorry, Grace. I can help you find a place."

Grace wiped at her eyes and shifted on her feet. "Thanks. That would be great. But I had another idea, and if I had options, I wouldn't ask you. Do you think we could stay in the carriage house?"

The carriage house was located behind the main house. Jesse hadn't renovated it fully. It was clean but in need of repairs throughout. "It's not in great shape."

"I could help you fix it up. Any work I do, you could deduct it from the rent."

Jesse ran his hands through his hair. He wasn't interested in being a landlord, and with the shooting fresh on his mind, he didn't like the idea of Grace being close. "We had a shooting here. I don't know if the farm is a safe place for you and Noah."

"I don't think the shooting had anything to do with

you. I can't imagine someone being that angry with you. I've heard rumors that the Alphabet Killer already took her *G* victim. That lets me off the hook, and I don't say that flippantly. I was worried."

Jesse hadn't heard about another victim in the case, but he was relieved Grace was safe, at least, for now. "You can stay in the carriage house after I've inspected it and made a few more repairs. If I don't have it ready in time, you and Noah can sleep here. I have a guest room you can share, and we can manage for a few days." He liked his privacy, but what choice did he have? He'd get the carriage house fixed and ready as soon as possible.

Grace rushed at him and hugged him. "Thank you, Jesse. I know this is putting you out, but you're saving me."

"Sure, sure," he said, already composing a list of to-dos for the carriage house. He wasn't afraid to get his hands dirty, and Grace had been a good employee and friend. He wanted to help her out. She reminded him of his mother. Good heart, bad circumstances, but made the best of it. If someone had been nicer to his mother, cut her a break, given her a chance, it would have lightened her load.

"I also wanted to tell you I heard something about Dylan Morris," Grace said.

That captured his full attention. "What about him?"

"Dylan and his girlfriend spend a lot of time at The Wet Whistle in Rosewood."

Jesse would go on a stakeout of his own at The Wet Whistle. "Thanks, Grace. I'll check it out."

"Does your interest in Dylan Morris have anything to do with the police officer who's been hanging around?" Grace asked, waggling her eyebrows.

He wouldn't lie to Grace. "Dylan's in trouble with the law, and he's directing his anger at the GGPD and one officer in particular."

Grace frowned. "Be careful around Dylan. He's unpredictable. When he worked here, I went out of my way to avoid him."

"I was worried about hiring him. It was the busy season, and I needed warm bodies." Jesse was usually more careful about the men and women he hired to work on the farm. Dylan had been strange, but Jesse had believed him harmless.

Grace absently touched her stomach. "Just be careful, okay? I know you want to help, but I don't want to see you get hurt."

"I will be. I know how to handle hotheads like Dylan," Jesse said.

He said goodbye to Grace and left the house planning to start his chores. Annabel was in her car. He should tell her about Dylan Morris and The Wet Whistle. When he arrived at her car, it pleased him slightly that she appeared bored.

"I have a lead on Dylan. I'm planning to talk to him."

Annabel straightened in her seat. "Without me?"

"You don't need to be involved."

Annabel screwed up her face. "Don't need to be

involved? Of course I'm involved. He's threatening me. I don't let others fight my battles."

This was one fight that might go better without her. Dylan Morris seemed to have taken the incident with Annabel personally. Dylan hadn't gone after her partner, who had also been involved in the arrest. She should be wary. But Annabel was headstrong. He recognized it in her because he could be the same way. "If you want to go, I'm heading out tonight."

"Heading where tonight?"

"He hangs out at The Wet Whistle in Rosewood. I'll leave around six."

"Never heard of it," Annabel said.

"I wouldn't expect you to. It's a dive. Sketchy characters hanging out, eating greasy food and drinking cheap beer. If you show up, the place will catch a whiff of cop, and everyone will scurry like rats."

"I can hide my cop side. I'll stop home and change and meet you here?"

Jesse shrugged, but his heart beat faster thinking of her being with him. He'd protect her, but he also enjoyed the idea of being alone with her, on their time, without her uniform between them. "I can follow you to Granite Gulch, and we can drive together to Rosewood."

She nodded her agreement.

When it was time to quit for the day, Annabel drove to Granite Gulch in her squad car, and Jesse followed in his truck. She parked outside Mia's place and motioned for him to come inside.

Jesse wasn't sure about going inside her friend's

place, but he was curious. He followed Annabel in. It was small and bright, neat except for the couch, which was piled with a pillow, sheets and a blanket. He pointed to the sofa. "Your bed?"

"For a while. The insurance company is working on longer term accomodations. Give me a minute to change. I'll be right down."

Jesse watched her take the stairs and wished she had invited him to go with her.

Annabel couldn't let Jesse speak to Dylan Morris alone. She let her sergeant know she had ended her shift a couple hours early to follow a lead on Dylan Morris. Though she'd have to answer questions in the morning, she needed to do this now. Regina wouldn't show up at Willard's Farm, but Dylan might be at The Wet Whistle.

Changing out of her uniform, she tossed it into the laundry basket. She looked through Mia's closet twice, and she decided she was spending too much time thinking about her clothes. She grabbed a black dress Mia swore worked anywhere and slipped it on. Adding a blazer and a pair of heels, a size too tight, Annabel grabbed an empty handbag from Mia's closet, her handgun and tossed in her wallet and keys.

Remembering her hair, she took it out of its ponytail and brushed it several times. It was long and loose around her shoulders, and while it would get on her nerves after a couple of hours, she would blend with a bar crowd.

She hurried down the stairs. Jesse was sitting on

the couch, facing the television, but it wasn't turned on. He stood when she stepped into the room. His jaw slackened. "Wow, Annabel, you look fantastic."

"Thank you. I was shooting for blending. It's Mia's dress, since all of mine smell like ash."

"If you want to blend, then throw a poncho over that, because that dress is smoking."

This wasn't a date. Annabel would make that her mantra for the evening. It didn't matter what compliments Jesse paid her; this was part of her investigation. She wanted to find Dylan Morris, arrest him and bring him in for questioning.

"I don't dress up often," she said.

"Why not?" he asked. "What else is there to do in Granite Gulch on a weekend except hit the bars?"

Lately, her weekends had been spent with Regina's letters to Matthew Colton and the investigation. "I work most weekends, and when I'm not working, I'm hanging out with my family, which has become less frequent of late. One by one, my brothers are finding the loves of their lives, and for some reason, they would rather spend time with them instead of with me." She cracked a smile. It sometimes made her feel lonely and left out to see her brothers happy. They had a secret silent language with their significant others. Annabel could read her twin Christopher well, but it wasn't a soul-deep connection like that of Sam and Zoe, Ethan and Lizzie, and Ridge and Darcy.

"You don't sound like a loser. You sound like a woman who needs a night out."

Jesse came closer, and she could smell his after-shave. He had stubble along his jawline, enough to make him look sexy and rugged. Rugged did something for her. She ran a hand down his shirt, stopping at his belt, tempted to let her hand wander farther south. Annabel was already walking in a gray area with her work by looking for Dylan Morris. Her sergeant hadn't been thrilled with the idea but had stopped short of forbidding it. She couldn't add a relationship with Jesse Willard to that list. The chief would be annoyed and her brothers furious. "Tonight isn't that night. Tonight is a work night."

"Let's beat feet," he said, his voice husky.

Neither of them moved. The only light in the room was from a lamp near the front window. "I can drive," she said, the words coming like a whisper. Maybe if she drove, it would feel less like a date.

"Allow me."

His mouth came down on hers, and she melted against him. His lips were the right combination of firm and soft, and she reached into his hair, threading her fingers through those blond locks, holding his mouth to hers. He moved his hand to her hip, and she wiggled, wanting his hand down, around, cupping her against him.

The need was strong, and she moaned, thinking of shoving him onto the couch and kissing him relentlessly.

He slipped his hand around to her backside, and she felt the tickle of fabric as her dress inched up her thighs.

Then his hand was cupping her bare bottom, his thumb brushing the fabric of her lace thong.

Grabbing the collar of his shirt, she spun him around and pushed him against the couch.

"I'm waiting for you to stop me," he said.

She climbed on top of him, aware of her skirt hiking up her thighs. Thank God Mia was working late tonight, preparing for the weekend rush. "I'm not finished yet."

She kissed him, their tongues dueling, her heart pounding and her body urging her to take him hard and fast. She'd never felt this level of passion for a man. Her body was on fire, and she wanted Jesse here and now.

Her hair fell forward, and Jesse brushed it over her shoulder.

She was a killer's daughter. Her father was a monster. It had taken her a long time to understand the darkness inside her father did not sleep inside her.

Jesse hadn't pretended to be unaware of her legacy. He hadn't minced words. He, too, had a blood relative who was a killer. Was that their bond? It was ice water on her desire.

She broke away, her breath coming in pants. She shoved her hair away. Matthew Colton ruined everything.

"What did I do?" he asked.

She didn't want to talk about Matthew or Regina. She had accepted who she was and where she had come from, but this was new to Jesse. "We need to find Dylan Morris."

"Normally, I would be insulted you were thinking of another man while kissing me, but I'll let it pass." Then he stroked his knuckles lightly down her cheek in a gesture that was warm and gentle and akin to affection. That gesture meant more than the kisses. It communicated more than words could have.

He cared about her. The realization sent shock waves over her. Had a man, aside from her brothers, ever cared about her? She'd had men want to get in her pants. She'd even dated a couple of wackos who had been turned on that Matthew Colton was her father. One had even asked for serial-killer memorabilia for his online museum.

But Jesse was different. He was the first man in a long time who'd come into her life who was good to her and seemed to have no agenda about it.

The Wet Whistle in Rosewood pulsed with country music audible from the parking lot. Annabel checked her gun again in the car and slid it into her handbag. She had cleaned it the day before, and she was prepared to use it. "Ready?"

"Let's not turn this into a shoot-out," Jesse said, glancing at her handbag.

"I have my gun for protection. It's not my goal for a situation to turn violent. I promise I will only pull out my weapon if I think it is absolutely essential, and I will only use it if I have no other options."

They stepped out of the truck and walked into the bar.

Jesse slid his arm around Annabel in a gesture

that felt natural and proprietary. In a place like this, it wasn't a bad idea to make it clear she was with Jesse. It might keep away unwanted attention. Annabel didn't want trouble unless his name was Dylan Morris.

Then she had questions to ask and a score to settle.

She and Jesse moved through the crowd, looking for Dylan. After circling the bar twice, Annabel hadn't seen him, and disappointment plucked at her.

Jesse leaned close to her ear. "I don't see Dylan, but I see someone who looks familiar. Maybe a friend of his." He pointed discreetly in the direction of the booths lining the far wall. "Let me do the talking, okay?"

Annabel nodded. She'd let Jesse lead the way. As they walked toward the booth, Annabel kept her eyes open and scanned around her.

"Hey, man," Jesse said, reaching across the table and clasping hands with a sullen-looking man in his late thirties with dark hair and squinty eyes. It was as if he was trying to calculate thirteen times fifteen in his head and couldn't get the answer.

"What are you doing around these parts?" the man asked. He glanced at Annabel, giving her a quick up-and-down assessment.

Annabel refused to squirm. She didn't like how he was looking at her, but she'd pretend she was accustomed to men eyeballing her in bars.

"Looking for Dylan," Jesse said.

The men at the table exchanged glances. Annabel watched them closely, hoping they'd give something away.

"He's not here tonight. He's been spending a lot of time at the Water Buffalo."

The men guffawed, and Annabel knew she was missing something.

"What's at the Water Buffalo?" Jesse asked.

"A nice pair of legs and a great set of…" The man's voice trailed off, glancing at her.

At least they were polite enough to realize when they were crossing the line into crass.

"My girlfriend and I are going to grab some drinks. I'll send over a round of beers," Jesse said.

The men lifted their glasses. "See you 'round, Jesse."

Jesse set his hand on her lower back and escorted her to the bar. After asking the bartender to bring a pitcher of beer to Dylan's friends and put it on his tab, Jesse pulled Annabel into his arms and on to the dance floor.

"They'll tell Dylan I was asking about him," Jesse said.

"We could go to the Water Buffalo," Annabel said. "See if we can catch him."

"They've already messaged him, and if he was there, he's likely already gone. We'll wait a couple of nights and then check it out. Let him think I gave up on it. They aren't smart enough to put together why I'd want to talk to him."

Jesse moved her around the dance floor, his powerful thighs brushing her legs.

"We could head back to Granite Gulch," Annabel said, liking the idea of being alone with Jesse. If they couldn't find Dylan tonight, at least they could salvage the night with some fun. Bars weren't Annabel's jam, but time alone with Jesse certainly was.

Jesse loosened his grip but didn't release her completely. "Is that what you want to do?"

She felt as if she was in another time and place, and all that mattered was her and Jesse. Here she was in his arms, and that felt good. "We can stay longer. We drove all this way."

As they danced, the song changed, and Annabel shifted, sliding one of her feet between Jesse's and laying her head on his shoulder. Her breasts were pressed to his muscular chest, and she felt her nipples pebble against her bra.

Why did the man of her dreams have to be involved in a case? Not just any case, but the most high-profile investigation in Granite Gulch since her father's.

"What are you doing tomorrow?" she asked.

"Working. Why?"

"It's my day off. I was planning to visit Luis at home, but then I have the rest of the day free."

"Are you volunteering to work with me?" Jesse asked.

"What if we snuck away from work?" She kissed the underside of his jaw. He groaned.

"Tempting, but I have a huge project that's time sensitive."

Disappointment speared her. She knew spring was

a busy time for farmers. Could she convince him that she would be worth procrastinating for? She ran her hand down his side and brushed her fingers across the front of his jeans. "How time sensitive? Because I feel like I'm about to go off."

He shuddered. "You're killing me, Annabel. If I hadn't promised a friend I would help, I would take the day to spend with you."

"What's going on?" she asked, wondering if she could assist him. He sounded serious, and maybe they could get the project finished faster and move on to free time alone.

"Grace is staying with her sister, but needs a place to live. She'll move in with me until I get the carriage house fixed up for her."

Hearing he would be living with another woman sent jealousy washing over her. "Grace is moving in with you?"

"Yes, with Noah. It will be a tight fit. He's a growing boy. He needs space."

"She can't live in an apartment?" Annabel asked.

"It's complicated," Jesse said.

"Is your relationship with her complicated?" She heard her voice getting shrill and took a deep breath. Why was this getting to her? Jesse had already told her that Grace was a good friend.

"My relationship with her is not complicated. Her situation is a mess. Can you keep a secret?" Jesse asked.

Wondering if her interest in Jesse was about to take a nosedive, Annabel leaned in. "Tell me."

"Grace is pregnant. The baby's father is a louse. She has no place else to go. So, yeah, she and her son are moving in with me until I can make sure the carriage house is safe for them."

Warmth and affection mixed in a potent brew. She had been letting the other woman bother her, and now she felt silly and ashamed for assuming the worst. "You are a good man."

He glanced away, some color in his cheeks. "I try."

"Let me help you tomorrow at the carriage house. I'll recruit my brothers to give us a hand. We can have that place livable for Grace and her family in no time."

"I don't think your brothers, at least Sam and Trevor, have time for that," Jesse said.

"Maybe not. But everyone can spare time now and then to help someone else. My family has a terrible legacy to overcome. The only way to do that is to spread as much kindness as possible."

"You are something else," Jesse said.

"Something good?"

"Definitely good. Too good. Irresistible," Jesse said.

It was her turn to blush. Heat poured over her, sizzling and thick. What she wanted to do with Jesse could not be done in public. "What do you think? Ready to go?"

Jesse nodded, taking her hand. He paid his tab and then hurried out of the bar and into his truck. When they were inside, Jesse reached for her. He kissed her, his passion sweeping over her, her excitement escalating.

The longer he kissed her, the more she ached for him to touch her. His hands were impossibly gentlemanly. "I would invite you back to my place, but it's uninhabitable," she said.

Jesse leaned back in the driver's seat. "Making out in the car does have a certain teenage quality to it. I'll drive you home."

Annabel squeezed his thigh. "Okay, if that's what you want to do."

"It's not what I want to do, but I get the sense this will work better if we take it slow."

It had taken all her life to meet someone like Jesse. Maybe he had the right idea about slow. Until the Alphabet Killer was caught, it was better for them to be uninvolved.

But the more time she spent with Jesse, the harder that was.

Chapter 9

At eight in the morning, three cars pulled into Jesse's driveway. Annabel and her siblings had arrived to help him with the carriage house. In their hands were toolboxes, picnic baskets and pitchers.

Annabel lifted the picnic basket as she approached. "We don't work hungry. Provisions."

"That's mighty kind of you," Jesse said.

"We're happy to help."

Jesse had driven out to the hardware store at six that morning to buy supplies and had hauled them to the carriage house. He'd unloaded them onto the porch. He sensed he'd need many more trips to the store before the project was complete.

Annabel introduced him to his helpers for the day: her brother Chris, her brother Ridge, and her friend

Mia. Jesse liked them and was grateful they were willing to help.

Trevor and Sam were noticeably absent. Perhaps they didn't want to lend him a hand. Despite his efforts to be amenable with the police and the Coltons in particular, they hadn't moved past the rough spots.

Jesse led them to the carriage house. He had his truck parked close to the entrance, the bed of the vehicle empty. "I have a lot of demo to do today. I don't know how much Annabel told you, but my friend Grace will be living here with her son. The goal is comfort and safety."

The Coltons and Mia nodded and moved into the house. Jesse explained what needed to be torn out and taken down. They got to work right away, and Jesse admired their work ethic. They were quick and focused, and they seemed in good spirits. After they removed some old, rotted cabinets in the kitchen, Jesse found Annabel carrying a cracked bathroom mirror to his truck.

"How's it going?" Jesse asked, taking one side of it.

They set the mirror in the truck, and Annabel wiped at the sweat on her forehead. "It bodes well for us that the house is small. But it's a nice place. I think Grace and her son will like it when it's done."

He agreed. It was a cozy place for a small family. "I have an electrician and plumber coming tomorrow to take a look at the systems in the house. They'll let me know exactly how nice of a place it is." He worried the house would need extensive work.

Annabel smiled and glanced to her left. Grace was walking in their direction carrying a pie in her hands. She stepped up onto the porch, and the scent of apple and cinnamon wafted from her dessert. "Hot apple pie. It's the least I can do to thank you," Grace said. "It's nice that you all came out to help me and Noah."

"We're happy to help a neighbor," Annabel said.

"Especially if it means homemade pie," Ridge said, coming outside carrying some rotted pieces of wood. He tossed them into the back of the truck.

Grace looked overcome with emotion. "That just means the world to me. I didn't believe the rumors I heard about the Coltons." She blushed and looked away. "That was rude. I meant I don't think families should pay for each other's mistakes."

Annabel patted her shoulder. "It's all right. We know what Matthew Colton did hurt a lot of people. I think about it every day."

Ridge nodded his agreement. "We've got pretty thick skin."

Grace smiled and went inside, announcing she had pie. The herd of footsteps told Annabel that Christopher and Mia were thrilled.

By four o'clock in the afternoon, the Coltons were dusty, grimy and tired. Cabinets had been tossed, rotted flooring torn up and broken railings, doors and hardware removed.

"How long do you think it will take to have this place in shape?" Annabel asked.

"At least a month."

"That's a long time to live with Grace and her son."

Jesse took off his red ball cap and scratched his head. "I know. I haven't lived with a woman before in my adult life. It will take some getting used to."

"If you need to get away, I know a place in Granite Gulch that's normally pretty quiet."

"Are you inviting me to Mia's?" he asked.

"Could be." She smiled, and lust tightened in his body. He wanted Annabel Colton. Their families were a big problem standing between them, but it didn't dissuade his desire.

As the Coltons and Mia were packing to leave, four of his farmhands were walking toward the carriage house.

Jesse met them in front of the house. "Everything okay?"

"Everything's fine," Tom said, stealing a glance at Grace, who was chatting with Mia.

"We're finished for the day. Mind if we give you a hand?" said another.

Jesse glanced at the carriage house. "With this? This is a personal project. Not farm business."

Tom shrugged. "We heard. We want to do this for Grace and Noah. We want to help."

Jesse wouldn't turn them away. "Please, I appreciate anything you can do. Thanks, guys."

The others moved into the house. Jesse was bowled over by their willingness to do more physical labor after the long day on the farm. They worked hard and deserved a break. Grace had won their loyalty and friendship.

Tom stood next to Jesse. "We heard what happened

to Grace, and she told me about the baby. That's not right. We want to do this for her."

Jesse heard something in Tom's voice and knew he cared deeply for Grace. Jesse tried to keep apprised of his farmhands, getting a sense of who worked well together and if any trouble was brewing. He had detected that Tom had a crush on Grace, but he wondered if more wasn't at play.

Jesse walked to his house, thinking about a night in front of his computer with his receipts. He tried not to focus on the slowing business or that the past two months of receipts had been terrible, especially for this time of year.

"What's the matter?" Annabel asked, jogging to join him.

"I have to do the worst part of my job tonight. The books," Jesse said.

Annabel winced. "That's not a task I enjoy either."

"I usually think of it as a necessary evil, but lately, expenses are up and sales are down, making it depressing, too."

The rumors about Regina had affected his business, no way around that. But Jesse didn't know how to change it.

"Have you thought about having a booth at the Spring Fling?" Annabel asked.

"I have." A few times over the past several years, he'd tried roadside stands and farmers' markets, but he didn't make enough money to justify the extra work.

"What if you asked Grace to handle the selling?

She's a good-looking woman, and she's charming. It might help. The Spring Fling has been setting up for weeks, and other farmers are registered. I even overheard some of them talking about making it a weekly event over the summer. Not the whole festival, but the produce, getting it in the hands of residents faster and easier."

It wasn't a bad idea. "I'll ask Grace what she thinks. Might win some new customers and help people to see we're not a family of psychopaths."

"Anyone who's met you knows you're not a psychopath."

He arched his brow. "Tell that to your brothers."

Annabel let out a bark of laughter. "Sam and Trevor want the Alphabet Killer found. They give me a hard time about my reports related to the killer. Don't take their hard attitude to heart."

Annabel followed him into the house.

Jesse grabbed two beers from the refrigerator and handed one to her. "Thanks to you and your family, I'm weeks ahead of where I thought I would be on the carriage house. And my team volunteering to help. On one hand, no surprise. We get to be like family. But it's rough work piled on top of a day of rough work."

"My brothers and Mia were happy to help. I feel like we have to go out of our way to prove we're good people."

"I understand that. Having something to prove."

She took a drink and then set it on the counter. "That's really good after a long day. I used muscles today I haven't in years."

She looked beautiful in his kitchen, her long dark hair in a braid down her back, the sunlight from the windows shining on her.

Jesse crossed to where she was standing. They had gone this far before, and he wanted to know if she'd go there with him again. She lifted her arms and linked them around his neck.

"Sounds like I owe you a massage in return for your help today," he said.

"As long as you don't make my brothers that offer, then I accept."

He laughed. "I don't give rubdowns to dudes."

"Good to know. Tell me what else is on your mind. There are creases around your eyes. Is it just the carriage house? Or the finances worrying you?"

At the moment, he wasn't concerned about the carriage house or the farm's accounts. "A beautiful woman is in my kitchen, and that means I have a lot of ideas on my mind. None of them related to remodeling or money."

She waggled her eyebrows. "Want to show me?"

Their mouths fused together in a tangle of tongues and heat. She speared her fingers into the back of his hair and tugged, just a little. He liked it. His desire had reached its boiling point. He grabbed her waist and lifted her onto the counter, bringing her eye level with him. Pushing her thighs apart, he stood between them and kissed her with everything he had.

"Wrap your legs around my waist," he said.

She did as he asked, and he lifted her, holding her

under her rear end and carrying her up the stairs. First stop was the bathroom.

He set her on the bathroom counter and left her briefly to turn on the shower.

Then he resumed kissing her. As the room filled with steam, he peeled her shirt over her head and let it drop to the floor. She was wearing a pink lace bra, and his pants grew tighter. Her flat stomach disappeared into the jeans. "You make work clothes look impossibly sexy," he said.

"I'm lucky that dusty and sweaty turns you on."

She turned him on. In whatever she was wearing and whatever she was doing. "I see a hardworking woman who needs some stress relief. I can help with stress relief. A stroke here—" he brushed her side "—and a touch here—" he let his hand drift between her legs "—and we'll both be feeling great in no time."

He removed her shoes and then her socks and finally unsnapped and unzipped her pants. Shifting her on the sink, he slipped his hand into her pants and found her wet and hot.

He groaned, thinking how much he wanted to be pounding inside her. He had to be patient. Annabel deserved more than frantic sex. This meant more than a quickie in his bathroom. He couldn't say how he knew this was the beginning of something, but he was certain of his feelings for Annabel and one time wouldn't be enough.

She slid off the counter and shimmied out of her pants. As if doing a dance, she kicked them away. She was crazy hot in her bra and pink underwear, and he ached to touch her. Turning toward the counter and giving him her back, she unclasped her bra and let it fall. Those thin straps of fabric moving down her arms were captivating.

He removed his shirt and pants and opened the door to the shower. Steam billowed out. He stepped inside, standing under the spray for a few seconds, and extended his hand to her. She took it, removed her panties and then moved under the hot spray with him.

He soaped them both, their slick skin slipping together as they touched and caressed. His shampoo was on the bench in the shower. Annabel poured some into her hands, reached up and rubbed it into his hair. Her fingertips massaged his scalp, and her breasts pressed into his chest. The scent of his shampoo, crisp and clean, surrounded them.

His erection found a place between her thighs, rubbing back and forth, but not entering her.

If he didn't slow down and stay calm, he would finish before they started. He rinsed the soap out of his hair, and then he turned her, letting her hair get wet. He knelt on the floor of the shower and lifted her right foot, setting it on the bench.

He ran a finger between her legs, slowly, testing her reaction. She closed her eyes and moaned, reaching for the wall to steady herself. Jesse kissed her in the most intimate way, letting his tongue move up and down, using his hands to excite her. Long licks alternated with flicks of his tongue, and her hips began to move against his mouth.

She held him against her, twisting his hair around her fingers. Her hips bucked hard against his mouth, and he tasted her, loved the noises she was making, every twitch of her body urging him to keep going.

Then she shouted his name as she came, her leg dropping to the shower floor. She collapsed onto the bench, resting her head against the wall. He kissed her thigh, her stomach, her breasts and then her perfect mouth.

"My legs feel weak," she said.

"Then rest for a while. I'll wash your hair."

He drizzled shampoo in her hair and lathered the soap. She seemed more relaxed than he'd seen her before, and he loved that she was at ease naked with him. Completely out of uniform, she was a different woman. His woman. Confident and sexy and fun.

Jesse wasn't a possessive man, but having Annabel created emotions he hadn't expected. He wanted her. More than just for tonight. She challenged him, she infuriated him and she intrigued him. He liked being with her. Despite the complicated situation, she was easy to be with. He didn't need to say a lot, and he felt as if he'd known her for years.

She stood and rinsed her hair. White bubbles covered the shower floor, and the way she lifted her hands over her head and shook the water and soap from her hair was distinctly feminine. He enjoyed it immensely.

She opened her eyes and pivoted with a wicked smile on her face. "Your turn."

"You don't have to…" His arousal would go away.

She reached for the soap and rubbed it on her hands and then slid them up and down his shaft. Her total concentration seemed to be on the task. Feeling pressure building, he stilled her hands. "You're too good at that."

"Let me see if there's something else you'll enjoy." Letting the soap disappear down the drain, she knelt and brought him into her mouth.

The warmth and suction were perfect, and she moved him in and out, deeper and deeper. He expected to hit a point where she couldn't take him farther, but she gave him the greatest pleasure he'd known with a woman.

Adding her hand, she increased her pace, her cheeks hollowed and her jaw loose. The tightness in his body gave away what was coming next. He moved her off him, and he sprang free from her mouth with a pop. He braced his hand on the wall, and she finished him with her hand.

Now he was the one with weak legs. Leaving the shower running, he grabbed fresh towels from the linen closet. He wrapped one around his waist and waited for her to exit the shower.

She shut off the water and stepped onto the bath mat, her hair dripping and creating rivulets of water that turned him on. Jesse covered her in a towel, wrapping it around her shoulders.

"Feel better?" he asked.

She nodded and adjusted the towel to be around her midsection. He reached for a second towel from the closet and patted her hair.

"Do you have something clean I could borrow?" she asked.

"I'll find something." Going into his room, he brought her some sweatpants and a T-shirt. When they were dressed similarly, they lay in his bed, her wet hair on his pillow. His sheets and his pillow would smell like her.

"Let's go out tonight," she said, rubbing her cheek against his chest as they reclined together.

"What did you have in mind?" If she wanted dinner, they could change their clothes and drive to Fort Worth to a nice restaurant where they wouldn't run into anyone they knew. That freedom would allow her to not be a cop for the night and for him to not be the brother of a suspect in a serial-killing spree.

"The Water Buffalo." Those words brought back what they were involved in doing, and Jesse wished he could have stayed focused on his idea about dinner in Fort Worth. He was thinking about her as his girlfriend, but her intentions seemed to be elsewhere.

Was she blowing off steam with him? Did this mean anything aside from a romp in the shower?

Annabel wasn't his new woman. She was a police officer being terrorized by a former employee. She was working a serial-killer case in which his sister was a suspect.

Jesse wished they'd had more time without those matters wedging between them. It was a blast of cold air over the entire evening.

"I'd prefer we go somewhere nicer," he said, trying to play it off, wishing she would buy into tonight being about them and not about finding Dylan Morris.

Annabel kissed the underside of his jaw. "Tonight, the Water Buffalo. After we find Dylan Morris, we can go out, just the two of us, without worrying about him."

He couldn't say no to her. "If that's what you want to do, then I'll take you to Mia's to change and we'll go to the Water Buffalo."

The Water Buffalo Bar was located in Rosewood, on the far side of town, away from Granite Gulch. It was a remodeled two-story brick home, one side of the wall crumbling and the wood porch on the front sagging. A small sign lit in the window announced it was open.

The gravel parking lot was half filled with beat-up, rusted cars. The dumpster near the back of the parking lot was overflowing. Cigarette and cigar butts littered the ground around the porch.

"How is this place not a health-code violation?" Annabel asked.

"Maybe it's cleaner inside."

It was not better inside. As they entered the bar, Annabel was struck by the stink of stale tobacco and old beer permeating the air. This was a place where Dylan Morris voluntarily hung out?

On the walls were framed pictures of Fifties pinup girls in cowboy hats, boots and chaps and not much else. The women who worked in the bar were dressed similarly, though their hair and makeup were more modern.

Annabel looked around the bar. No sign of Dylan. The room narrowed by the bar, and additional tables were in the back. Dylan could be hanging out there. Was there an upstairs accessible to patrons? Annabel and Jesse walked through the bar, her shoes squishing on the grimy floor. She looked down and saw French fries and crunched potato chips. When was the last time the floor had been swept?

As they moved through the small room, Annabel tried not to make it obvious she was scrutinizing the patrons. Most sat with their heads lowered and their shoulders slumped toward the table. It was a depressing place.

The night was young, and there was the chance Dylan would still show up.

"We could wait and watch in the parking lot," Jesse said.

"That's okay. We can handle it here," Annabel said. "We don't know if Dylan has friends or if he'll come by."

"Grace confirmed he hangs out with his girlfriend here. She didn't know if the girlfriend works here or if she just enjoys the ambience." He gave her a wry grin.

"We'll watch and wait. If he shows up, I'll assess the situation, or call for backup," Annabel said.

They took a seat at an empty table near the back of the room. Their view of the front door would tell them if Dylan entered the room. The back room was empty except for five round tables. They could be too early to meet the regular crowd.

"You have experience on stakeouts. Tell me the tricks to making the time pass," Jesse said.

Annabel heard something in his voice, but before she could respond, a waitress sauntered over and Jesse ordered them two bottled beers, keeping his eyes on her face. That had to be difficult because she was worth staring at.

Annabel nodded her agreement to the order. The beer was likely the best drink they served.

"Are you planning to give me a hard time about that?" Annabel asked. Passing the time at the farm was a matter of keeping her thoughts occupied. Being with Jesse was not the same challenge. She enjoyed talking to him.

"Doesn't it get boring sitting outside my farm, watching and waiting for something that isn't going to happen?" Jesse asked.

Annabel didn't like the long hours, but police work was boring at times. "I like watching your crew. The farm is busy, and that makes the hours pass faster. To me, growing anything, especially growing entire fields of crops, is a form of magic. When I was growing up, one of my foster mothers had a garden. She spent hours on it every year. I was not blessed with a green thumb, and it seemed impossible." She and Mia had weeded Mama Jean's garden in the summers, and Mia had caught on to the planting. But Annabel had tried to grow herbs in small pots on her windowsill and had failed.

"With the right know-how and instincts, it's possible," Jesse said. "You'd be surprised how much I rely on science to resolve problems."

She must have zero gardener instincts. "Did you always want to be a farmer?"

Jesse shook his head. "I thought I would walk away from small-town life. I dreamed of going to college and getting a job in the financial sector, carrying a leather briefcase and wearing a suit."

The picture he painted was the opposite from the man sitting in front of her. She couldn't imagine Jesse in a suit. He looked too good in jeans and a plaid shirt. "What changed?"

"When I was in high school, a friend's father hooked me up with a job in New York City, working on Wall Street. I hated it. I hated the crowds and the noise and the smog. The work itself was boring. I felt trapped in a Freon prison."

She laughed. "That bad?"

"I finished out the summer at the financial firm and came home to Texas. Home was open space and working with my hands and being outside. I was looking to fill a void. I thought a different life from how I had been raised would make me happy. Turns out, apple doesn't fall far from the tree."

Questions sprang to mind, but asking about his childhood could mean bringing up Regina, a sensitive topic. They had spent the better part of the evening in each other's arms, but Annabel didn't know where the line was. They were having fun, but she was still a police officer. "Are you worried you'll end up like your father?" Jesse had mentioned before that his father was not a good man.

The waitress brought their beers, and Jesse took a swig of his. "I didn't know him well enough to know why he was angry with the world. He had a temper on a hair trigger. I doubt I would turn into him. Too much I love about my life."

"What about your mother? Are you more like her?"

Jesse shot her a strange look, as if he didn't want to discuss the matter. "Nicest woman, but her biggest flaw was she couldn't see people for who they were. She saw them for who she wanted them to be."

Was he implying the same applied to their relationship? "Rose-colored glasses?"

"Yes. The only saving grace in her life, and maybe in mine, was when she met my stepfather. He was mild-mannered, patient and loving. When my mother and I ran from my father, we were scared of him finding us. For the longest time, we moved every few months, trying to stay one step away from him. When we met Frank, it changed our lives. He was a good man. Worked in a supermarket and worked hard. He earned my trust, and he never raised a hand to my mother. He only raised his voice to her once that I can remember, and that was because she told him that my father might come looking for us. Frank told my mother that he could come, but he wouldn't get close to either of us. Frank kept his promise."

Annabel was glad to hear Jesse had a happy family life after the disappointments he had experienced with his biological father.

"I still call Frank from time to time. He remarried five years after my mom died, but he treats me like a son. He invites me to visit, and I plan to take him up on it soon. What about you? What pulled you from your rough childhood and turned you into a cop?"

Trying to prove to the world she was a good person, feeling her father had done his family and his victims and their families wrong. She had wanted to make a positive difference in Granite Gulch. "I had a wonderful foster mother. We weren't together long, but long enough for her to show me the goodness inside people and believe that people wanted to do right. Despite what my father did, I believe most people are good and decent."

"That's a bold statement from someone who deals with criminals," Jesse said.

Some days, she didn't understand why people made the choices they did. "If I didn't believe in the inherent goodness of people, I don't think I could do this job," Annabel said.

The conversation flowed between them. Annabel enjoyed talking to Jesse. She liked his sense of humor, his insights and how well he listened.

When the bartender rang a bell over the bar and shouted for last call, disappointment swamped her. Annabel had wanted to find Dylan tonight. The one salve on the night was that, despite the location being among the last she would frequent on a night off, she'd had a nice time with Jesse.

Jesse paid their tab and they exited the bar, waiting in Jesse's car with the lights off on the chance Dylan would still show up. The bar and parking lot emptied, and the sign in the front window went dark.

Jesse leaned across the seats and pressed a kiss to her lips. "I've wanted to do that all night."

His lips lingered near hers. Annabel set her hand on the side of his face and kissed him. "Why did you wait so long?"

"The moment didn't seem right until we were alone. I didn't want to distract you from your stakeout. We were here on serious business."

Annabel ran her fingers down the side of his face. She kissed him again, a long, lingering kiss. Her stomach fluttered, and she wanted to move closer. The dashboard prevented her from maneuvering the way she wanted.

The glare of headlights turned into the parking lot. They froze. As the car passed, Annabel peered into it, hoping to see who was driving.

She couldn't see well enough to identify the driver. The car parked around the back of the tavern. A waitress came out of the back of the bar and climbed into the passenger seat.

"Was that Dylan's girlfriend?" she asked.

Jesse narrowed his gaze in the direction of the truck. "I don't know. Want me to stop them from leaving?"

Before she could answer, he was out of the truck, waving his hands above his head to get their attention. Annabel couldn't leave him to face Dylan alone.

Dylan could have a weapon. He had left a bomb at her house. He wouldn't think twice about shooting a civilian. Annabel hopped out of the car and ran after him.

Chapter 10

Jesse wandered to the driver's side of the truck. Annabel caught a glimpse of the driver. He wasn't Dylan Morris. "My wife and I are having some trouble remembering which is the way to Granite Gulch. Can you point us in the right direction?"

The man gave them a funny look but indicated turning to the left out of the parking lot. Jesse thanked him, and they hurried back to the car.

"I can't believe you did that! What if it had been Dylan?" Annabel asked.

"Then it would have been better for you to stay in the car. Dylan and I are not on great terms, but he wouldn't take a shot at me."

Annabel shivered. "Next time, we discuss the plan first."

"I was afraid they'd leave, and we'd miss our chance to find him. We drove out here, and I hate to return empty-handed."

The night hadn't been wasted. She'd had fun with Jesse. She moved closer to his seat and touched his arm. "Thank you for tonight. You don't have to do this for me."

Jesse grinned at her. "Sure I do. I'm a gentleman."

As they drove to Granite Gulch, Jesse turned on the radio. It played softly in the car, but Annabel didn't need music at all. The roads were quiet, and the sky was beautiful and she was with Jesse.

They were about five minutes from Willard's Farm when important questions sprang to mind. Would she spend the night with Jesse? She didn't want to over-stay her welcome, but going inside with Jesse held some interesting possibilities. Was their adventure that afternoon a one-time fling? Could it be more?

She wanted the answer to be yes, but what they had was limited by time and depth. Her brothers would only see him as Regina Willard's brother, and she had to maintain professional distance from him to remain objective about the case. Her ties to the investigation via her father were a definite gray area, and she couldn't complicate matters.

"I need to know something, and I'd like a straight answer from you," Jesse said.

The seriousness in his voice was different enough from his playful tone that she took note.

"I try to be straightforward with you," Annabel said.

"I know. Given that and what happened between

us, I feel like I can ask you this question. What has my sister done that convinces you she's the person you're looking for? Why do you believe she is the Alphabet Killer?"

A dozen answers sprang to mind. Regina's letters to Matthew Colton. Her abandoned boarding room in Rosewood. The connection between her job at the diner and her victims—those credit card receipts were terribly damning. Annabel wasn't sure how many details of the case were public. Speculation and rumors were rampant, but as a member of the Granite Gulch Police Department, it was her job to uphold the integrity of the investigation.

She checked every word before she spoke it. "The FBI crime lab has authenticated the letters from Regina to Matthew Colton came from her. In those letters, she strongly implicates herself." Regina hadn't written outright that she planned to kill anyone, but she had included details that tied her to the killings.

"How do you know Matthew Colton isn't playing a game? He could have fabricated those letters or tricked Regina into writing them and then provided it to the FBI out of context. From what I hear, he's pretty twisted."

It had been a long time since a negative comment about her father hurt her, but hearing Jesse say it, it burned like an old injury that ached when it rained. "That could be true. Matthew Colton has time, the intelligence and the means to toy with the people around him." But the FBI crime lab was certain the letters had been sent from outside the prison to Matthew. The prison logged incoming inmate mail and had records of Regina's letters with dates and times of arrival.

"Here's where I can't make the connection. Regina was good to me growing up. We didn't live together long, and I will always regret that she was left with our father, but you have to understand what she did for me. She protected me. From my father and from bullies in the neighborhood who made fun of us because we were poor and our clothes were too small and our shoes worn through. Regina was my one ally. She is the one person who knows what we went through and how hard it was."

Annabel's chest ached. The parallels in their story were striking. She often felt her brothers were the only people capable of understanding how it felt to be the child of a serial killer. "I'm sorry, Jesse. I know those memories must be precious to you, and I don't want to say anything to take them away. Even if Regina has changed, if she is someone else now, that doesn't mean she wasn't a good sister to you then."

"Is that how you feel about your father? He was a good father to you even though he killed all those people?"

Jesse didn't pull punches. Annabel felt herself struggling with her emotions. What she felt for Jesse was new and fresh and felt good, and talking about her father brought the opposite emotions. They collided inside her in a potent cocktail. "I do not think Matthew Colton was a good father. I do not think he is a good man. I don't know how someone can be so dark and twisted to do what he did, even though he had to realize the consequences. He hurt people without caring about their feelings. I remember a man who could be kind and sweet one minute and vicious and cruel the next. I think those sweet moments were manipulative, completely without sincerity. I have no good memories of my father. Not a single one that makes me feel sorry for him or wish he was in my life. Matthew Colton is a bad man, and I accepted it long ago."

Jesse pulled into the driveway leading to his house. He reached across and took Annabel's hand. "I'm sorry you've had to live with that. I can't imagine, as young as you were, how you coped."

She had been in denial after her mother had died. It had been difficult to accept her new reality, and nearly impossible to acknowledge her father was responsible. Annabel kept to the facts, the way Mama Jean had. Gently and kindly, but the facts without opinion and hearsay were easiest to understand. "There's something else I am reluctant to tell you about Regina."

"Why reluctant?"

"It's part of an ongoing investigation, and I care about your feelings."

"You don't have to spare my feelings. Tell me. Help me understand what makes you certain my sister is a monster."

He sounded angry, and Annabel didn't blame him. She couldn't guess Jesse's reaction. She didn't want to hurt him, but wasn't the pain inevitable? "The other day, my partner and I were called to assist with a reported crime. The victim had been attacked by the Alphabet Killer."

Jesse parked the car and turned off the motor and the lights. He faced Annabel, watching her, listening intently. At least she had that.

"The victim's first name began with *G*. She is the seventh victim of the Alphabet Killer who we know about. She was shot twice in the head and marked with the killer's signature. She was taken to Blackthorn County General, and we met her there to speak with her about what happened."

The next part was the hardest to say. "She identified Regina Willard as her attacker."

Several long beats passed. Annabel wouldn't fill the silence with nonsense. It was a lot for Jesse to take in.

"What happened to the woman?" Jesse asked. His voice was gravelly and the emotion raw and almost hard to hear.

"She did not survive the surgery." Whether it had taken too long to get to Blackthorn County General or her wounds were too great, Annabel didn't know. She had not been privy to the medical examiner's autopsy report. The last Annabel had heard, the FBI had confirmed Gwendolyn was a victim of the Alphabet Killer. The ballistics, the trace evidence and the methods fit.

Jesse turned away from her and looked straight out the front windshield. He said nothing, and his expression was unreadable. Annabel remembered what she had needed when her mother had died. She had needed a friend. Her brothers and sister had been taken from her, and she had needed someone to stay by her side. Words weren't as important. It had been nice to have someone around.

Jesse climbed out of the car. He circled to the passenger's side and opened it. He took her hand and helped her out onto the driveway. Though he was silent, she wasn't afraid. He was letting her know that he, too, needed a friend.

Hand in hand, they walked into the house. He greeted his dogs, fed them and poured food in the cat's bowl, as well. Then Jesse lifted Annabel into his arms and carried her up the stairs.

"Stay with me," he said. "I won't ask anything more of you. Just stay with me. I don't want to be alone tonight." His voice cracked, betraying the emotion swirling beneath.

Annabel hugged him. "I can do that."

She kicked off her shoes, and they lay together in the middle of his bed, their hands clasped together, staring at the ceiling.

Several hours passed. Though he barely moved, Jesse wasn't asleep.

"You must think I'm disgusting," he finally said.

His words were raw; they chafed her to the core. She remembered those same feelings. She had felt like less of a person because she was Matthew Colton's daughter. She had considered changing her last name, perhaps taking her mother's maiden name as her own, but she worried her siblings wouldn't find her. In the end, she had made good on being a Colton. She liked to think she had brought some honor back to the name. "Being the relative of a murderer does not reflect on you. I've studied criminology. I've studied criminal cases. People go off the rails. They make bad decisions, and they can't find their way back to good. They are consumed by anger and jealousy and greed, and it blights out everything right inside them. That doesn't mean anything about the family."

"You saw her victims. You saw what she did to them. Seven people. Seven deaths and I don't understand why. What good does it do to kill someone?"

It served no purpose. But Regina had something dark inside her, demons she couldn't excise. "She has her reasons even if they only make sense to her. She carries a lot of rage with her." Her letters to Matthew Colton had contained blame and anger for everyone in her life, for what they had done and what they had failed to do for her.

"You must think I'm an idiot for not seeing it. Or worse, you think it reflects on me."

He wouldn't make eye contact. Even in the dark, with the light of the moon shining through the windows of his bedroom, Annabel could read the devastation on his face. "Look at me. What do you see in my eyes?"

Jesse looked at her. Green eyes met blue ones. "You look sad."

"Sad because I've been where you are and I know it's hard. It feels terrible. Coming to terms with this and fully accepting it will take time. When you think of me, do you think of my father?"

He shook his head. "Only when you bring him up."

"My brothers and I are running as fast as we can to distance ourselves from that legacy. We're trying to prove we're more than Matthew Colton. We're not killers. We're not cold and soulless. We care about people."

"You're one of the warmest women I've ever known."

"Yet my father was one of the most brutal killers in Granite Gulch's recorded history. Maybe one of the most brutal killers who's lived in Texas."

"I don't know what to do now."

"Let me hold you. Let me show you that I care for you," Annabel said.

A tear slipped down his cheek, and he lifted his mouth to hers and kissed her. He was seeking a connection, and she would give it to him. She would be everything he needed tonight.

"Are you okay knowing Regina is a killer?" Jesse asked.

"I've suspected her since before we met. It hasn't stopped how I feel about you."

"How is that?" Jesse asked, brushing his hand down her hair.

"I like you. You're fun and sweet. I miss you when we're not together."

He kissed her softly on the lips. "I feel lost."

"Then let me be your guide. Let me show you there's a way out of this dark time."

Jesse kissed her again. "I feel desperate and exposed."

"You don't have to hide anything from me. You don't have to pretend to be anyone you're not. Let me make you feel good."

She accepted Jesse as he was. He was a good man, and she liked him. His hurt and grief were potent, and she wanted to comfort him.

Jesse moved over her, bracing his weight on his arms, and kissed her. She tasted his hunger and his desperation to have her, to have her on his side fully and completely.

Annabel closed her eyes, and he kissed each of her eyelids, then her mouth and lower to the top of her dress. He pulled the fabric to the side, trailing kisses along her collarbone. She arched underneath him, wanting to let him set the pace. His mouth turned her on and going slow was hard. Tonight would be about him and letting him take and have what he needed.

He cupped her breast and squeezed lightly. She had always wanted to be more endowed in that area, but Jesse seemed plenty fascinated, his gaze lingering on her bra a few minutes before he pulled the fabric cups down and sucked one pert tip into his mouth, his hand massaging the other. Then he switched sides and excitement jolted through her. Annabel stroked his hair, running her fingers through the soft strands.

He let out a growl when the top of her dress would not give further. She sat and peeled it over her head, tossing it to the ground.

Half-naked before him, she wrapped her arms

over her chest, feeling self-conscious. Earlier he had touched every inch of her in the shower, and she had felt amazing and sexy and bold. Now, they had a deep and meaningful connection, impossible to deny.

He took her arms and gently uncrossed them. "Don't. You're lovely. Every part of you, inside and out."

Had anyone called her lovely before? As a teenager, she had been in survival mode, defensive and hostile. When she had worked as a park ranger and then as a cop, she downplayed her femininity, knowing she would gain more respect from her peers and her brothers if she came across as hard and uncaring about her appearance.

Jesse made her feel feminine but also powerful. It was a sensation she enjoyed.

He covered her body with his, and she set to work on his shirt, unbuttoning the row down the front of the blue plaid, pushing it to the side to reveal the roped muscles beneath. Tanned skin and hard plains tapered to a ripped stomach.

Peeling the shirt over his shoulders, she reveled in his bare skin pressed to hers. He kissed her until she was mindless and dizzy, and then he reached between her legs, moving aside the fabric of her underwear, and slipped his fingers inside. She was tender and swollen from the afternoon in his arms, but the wetter she became, the easier his fingers slid between her folds, raising her anticipation.

He stared for a long moment at her. "Wow." The tone was filled with awe. He hooked his thumbs around her underwear and drew them down her legs. He dropped them and slid her to the edge of the bed, her legs dangling over the side of the mattress.

He set his hands on her knees, prodding her to open her legs wide.

She was suddenly nervous. They had done this before, and she had no reason to be, yet, this felt like so much.

"Relax," he said. He parted her thighs and brought his head between them.

His breath blew over her, and he stroked her inner thighs.

"You don't have to…" Her thoughts flew out of her head as his tongue pressed into her. His hands held her thighs open, and the heat of his mouth felt incredible. He tongued her, and within moments her entire body was engaged in what he was doing and loving it.

He was amazing at this. The right pressure and the motion, the steady pace, building her higher and higher. Her hips thrashed, and she wanted release, but she wanted him inside her when she finished.

"I can't come yet," she said.

He didn't respond and continued his assault. When completion washed over her, he slowed down and shifted her legs onto the bed. He drew the covers away and slid a pillow under her head.

Removing his pants, he climbed into bed with her. Spooning his body against hers, she felt his arousal between her thighs, but he made no motion to push inside her.

His hands brushed against her breasts, and he kissed the back of her neck.

She lifted her leg to give him access and found him long and hard, moving against the sensitive skin of her inner thigh.

"Wait, wait," he said. He reached behind him and pulled a condom from his night table. She heard the tearing of packaging and then the crinkle of the condom being rolled on.

She caught him in her hand and guided him toward her entrance. He pressed against her, his size impressive. Relaxing her muscles, her wetness gave him better access. Several thrusts and he was inside. Shifting her hips, she took him deeper, deeper, until she felt stretched and full.

He rocked his hips, working his length in and out. She controlled the depth of his pumps, her body oversensitive, the nerve endings between her legs tingling and hyperaware of every brush of his skin against hers.

Without pulling away, he lifted her onto her knees. He brushed her hair over her shoulder so he could see her face. Then he seated his body fully into hers. The angle and position made him feel bigger.

He moved slowly at first, holding her hips and using them for leverage. His thrusts were more insistent, and he reached between her legs to rub the bundle of nerves at her core. He moved like a piston, sinking inside her and pulling away, the friction amazing and the look on his face intense.

He grabbed a fistful of her hair and pulled lightly, her body accepting him as part of her, riding her hard.

Another orgasm crept over her and exploded around her before she could warn him.

He seemed utterly pleased with himself as he withdrew and turned her onto her back. "More?" he asked.

How was he still going? Her body felt tingly and relaxed. "Yes." She would take everything he had to give her. This had been about making him feel good and showing him she accepted him and everything about him, but she was having the best sex of her life.

He slid into her with swift precision. He palmed her breasts and surged hard. His hips snapped faster. He was close. She lifted her hands over her head and moaned. Everything felt good.

With a satisfied roar, he slammed inside her as he climaxed. He was panting and he buried his head in her neck, kissing her languidly.

As their heart rates returned to normal, he rolled to the side.

After several beats, he sat. "Give me a minute."

He went into the bathroom and returned, strutting naked across the room, the moonlight accentuating his muscled body, hard and primed from long days in the sun.

He slipped into bed next to her and slid his arm around her waist. Nuzzling her neck, he made a sound of satisfaction.

Annabel pulled the sheet over them, putting one of her legs between his and closing her eyes.

Jesse's even, deep breathing gave away he was

asleep. Sex had had a sedative effect on him. Though her body felt tired, her brain was running too fast.

Sex with Jesse had been mind-blowing. She didn't realize sex could be that good. Was this the type of connection they'd found with their significant others? She could see herself falling for Jesse, and she could see wanting more time with him. How could she sleep with him and walk away in the morning? She felt as if she had launched herself off an emotional cliff, and she was counting on Jesse to catch her.

Bliss gave way to darker thoughts. They crept over her and took hold. Her father had not believed she or her brothers were worth anything. He hadn't cared that his actions had torn apart their family. Her mother had died at his murderous hands. Her beloved foster mother, Mama Jean, had died of a heart aneurysm. Her brothers had been taken from her, and though they'd later reunited, their relationship had suffered from many years apart. They didn't accept her for who she was and believed she couldn't hack it as a police officer. Her sister, Josie, had disappeared.

Everyone in her life who was close to her was either taken from her or had suffered.

The past couldn't dictate the future, but it was a good predictor of what was to be.

Annabel rolled to look at Jesse. He was devastatingly handsome, charmingly rugged, and she was falling for him. The day he had swaggered into the police station, she had lost a piece of her heart to him.

Jesse seemed to accept his sister was the Alphabet Killer, but Annabel knew firsthand, when the information fully penetrated, he would struggle with it. He would have to find a new reality, a new way of living with that terrible information dangling over him, following him all this life.

He may do reckless things. Turn people out of his life. Shut down emotionally.

Annabel ran her hand down his beautiful face. Was she strong enough to go through this with him? Was she strong enough to hold on through the inevitable ups and downs?

History indicated she was not. She had not forgiven her father, and she still had a chip on her shoulder about her brothers. She was angry with Josie for running away and blocking her from her life.

What would she tell Chief Murray? That she had decided to shack up with the brother of the prime suspect in the Alphabet Killer murders? Her brothers would be livid when they found out.

Annabel was not capable of handling this. She could be there for Jesse now, but the case was building against his sister, and Regina would make a mistake and be found. Everyone in Texas was looking for her. When she was captured and charged, it would tear her and Jesse apart.

Her relationship with Jesse, which had seemed shiny and bright only a short time ago, was doomed to fail and leave them both with terrible scars. It was too good now. The only place the relationship could go was down.

Annabel would end it first, before she became more involved, before either of them got hurt.

Annabel climbed out of bed on silent feet and found her clothes in the dark. If Jesse woke, what would she say? Thank him for the great sex and then run? She texted Mia that she needed a ride.

She dressed and then hurried out of the house. She raced down the driveway. Feeling like a coward, but knowing she was doing everything she could to protect herself, she didn't look back.

Chapter 11

The drive from Willard's Farm to Mia's house hadn't cleared Annabel's head. Her thoughts were spinning, and she wanted to hide until the shame cloud dissipated. She had tossed and turned on Mia's couch all night. Sleep had eluded her. Around seven in the morning, she decided to head over to her house to take a few pictures. The insurance company had sent an assessor earlier in the week, but Annabel wanted to document the repairs needed. It seemed prudent but also occupied her time.

She drove to her house and parked. Since she and Jesse had blocked off the front with plywood, she walked around to the back of the house. She used her key to enter, feeling silly the door was locked. The damage to the house made it easy to gain entrance for anyone who wanted it.

Annabel took some pictures. Her furniture was ruined, wet from the firemen's hoses and damaged by the smoke. Annabel wasn't a deeply sentimental person, at least not about property. She'd had to move around too often as a child, dragging her possessions from home to home in a garbage bag and later in a secondhand suitcase she'd acquired.

She had wanted to live in a home that was truly hers, one she couldn't be removed from at another's whim. It was one of the reasons she had bought this house as soon as she'd scraped together a down payment. But once her name was on the deed, she hadn't settled in. Over time, her possessions had grown, but she wasn't attached to anything. Breaking old habits was hard.

She heard movement behind her, coming from the back door. Was it the house settling after the fire? Dylan Morris or Regina Willard following her? Annabel reached for her gun and then swore under her breath. She had left it at Mia's. She wasn't due into work until nine.

She was the police. Was this her opportunity to apprehend a criminal? Had someone been watching her?

She moved across the room and tucked herself behind the wall. Looking around the corner, she saw no one. She moved to the back of the house and peered out the window.

A slender woman with long, dark hair was running through her backyard.

Her build wasn't the same as Regina Willard's, and while Annabel couldn't be sure, a tightening in her gut told her it was Josie. Maybe she was being unreasonable and hoping for something she ached for—a happy reunion with her only sister.

She ran out into the yard. "Josie!"

The woman didn't stop, and Annabel gave chase. She could be chasing a figment of her imagination. "Josie!" If her neighbors heard her screaming outside in the early morning hours, they would think she had lost her mind.

Lost her mind like their father had. A sobering thought that Annabel brushed aside. She ran harder.

Annabel chased after the brunette, jumping a neighbor's chain-link fence and looking around. She circled the house and ran down the driveway.

Annabel looked left and right. She listened for the sound of feet pounding against the pavement. The brunette had disappeared. Emotion wrapped around her. Had it been Josie? Annabel was tired and burned out. Could she have imagined the brunette?

Annabel jogged back to her house, looking for an unfamiliar car or any sign of Josie. Why come to the house and run away?

When she arrived at her home, she walked onto the porch. If she waited here, would Josie return? Her foot kicked something, sending it skittering across the cement. It thumped lightly against the railing. Annabel spotted metal glinting in the sun. She knelt to retrieve it.

It was a gold heart charm. Annabel recognized it

immediately. Dizziness slammed into her. She had a charm just like it, a gift from their mother the Christmas before she had been killed. She and Josie had been given the same bracelets and had a few charms to go on it.

All but one of charms had been different, specific to their tastes and talents. The heart charm had been exactly the same. Their mother had said it was a special heart between a mother and her daughters, representing an indescribable and fully consuming love. Annabel hadn't thought about the bracelet in a long time, and she wondered if it had survived the fire.

Did Josie remember the charm bracelets and what their mother had said to them about the hearts? Why had she come to the house? Did she leave the charm on purpose to let Annabel know she had been there? Or had it been an accident?

Their brother Ridge had sworn he had seen Josie. Lizzie believed the same. Was Josie checking on her siblings? Looking for something? If she was making her presence known in their lives, was she hoping for a reunion?

Josie was in hiding, and Annabel hated to think poorly of her sister, but it could be any number of problems keeping her away. Annabel wished she could tell Josie that she didn't care about whatever Josie had done or how terrible Josie might believe her life or her actions were. Annabel just wanted her sister in her life.

She could forgive almost anything of a sibling. She

squeezed the charm in her hand. Like their mother's love, her love for her siblings had no bounds.

Jesse awoke knowing he was alone in his house. Annabel hadn't said anything about needing to work early in the morning. She hadn't left a note. She hadn't woken him to say goodbye.

He had been a hot mess the night before. Learning that his sister was the Alphabet Killer still rattled around his brain, not quite taking hold. It was as if he had read the information, but his brain hadn't accepted it.

He and Annabel had shared an incredible night of sex, and then she had disappeared. She had slipped away in the dark. She was embarrassed by his ties to Regina. Her family had overcome a terrible legacy. He couldn't blame her for not wanting to be involved closely with another crime, especially one similar to her father's murders. Annabel was a rookie cop. It hadn't escaped his notice that her brothers Sam and Trevor seemed to speak to each other, but they didn't include Annabel in their discussions. Annabel had to establish her reputation as a good police officer. Rising above the rumors was hard enough, but to cast doubt over them by being involved with him made it impossible.

That thought was salt in a fresh wound.

Though Jesse hadn't had enough sleep and his head felt foggy, he put in an hour of work on the carriage house. As he entered, he was shocked to see the progress his farmhands had made. As if in answer to his silent question, he heard the squeak of a paint roller and strode to the kitchen.

Tom was painting the last wall in the room. New flooring had been laid, the cabinets were up, and baseboards and trim had been replaced.

"Nice work," Jesse said.

Tom set the paint roller in the pan and wiped his forehead. "Grace and Noah are staying with her sister. It's a ticking clock. If I can get her kitchen, bathroom and bedrooms ready, this place will be livable."

"I wasn't expecting you to do the work," Jesse said, surprised at how intent Tom looked.

"I know. We all know this isn't for you or about our work. It's kind of you to help Grace, and we've been pitching in. She's a good person, and she deserves a break."

"That's nice of you to do this," Jesse said.

Tom returned to rolling paint on the wall. If he didn't want to talk about his feelings for Grace, that was fine with Jesse. He had woman troubles of his own. "I'll be in the upstairs bathroom taking care of some plumbing tasks," Jesse said.

Jesse took the stairs, noting they needed to be sanded and refinished, and started the plumbing in the bathroom.

As he worked, his mind wandered, first to the farm, then Annabel, his bills, Annabel, his sister and then Annabel again. She had gotten under his skin, and it bothered him that she had left in the middle of the night. Having thicker skin about these matters would help, but he couldn't stop his feelings for her.

He had opened up to her and bared his soul, and she had slept with him and then run away. He was on his own, as he had been most of his life.

Annabel arrived at the precinct early. She wanted to talk to Sam about seeing Josie at her place and what it could mean.

Sam was at his desk working on his computer, and Annabel pulled a chair next to his. "I think I saw Josie this morning."

Sam stopped typing and turned his head to look at her. "Say that again."

"I think I saw Josie this morning. At my house. I went over to take some pictures of the damage, and I heard a noise. I went to the back porch, and I saw a woman who looked like Josie running away."

Sam swiveled his chair toward her. "How do you know it was Josie and not some neighbor's kid poking around? We don't know what Josie looks like."

Annabel reached into her pocket and withdrew the charm. "If it was a neighbor, then they had the heart charm that Mom gave me and Josie."

Sam looked at the charm in her palm. "Where did she go?"

"I tried to follow her. I ran after her, calling her name, but I lost her. Why would she come to my house and then run away before I could talk to her?"

"I don't know. It's what Ridge and Lizzie reported, too. Annabel, I'm sorry. That's terrible," Sam said. It was an unusual display of compassion.

Tears sprang to her eyes. She blinked them away. "She's in Granite Gulch. We need to find her."

Sam rubbed his jaw. "Resources are tight. We don't have anyone extra to spare for nonemergency searches."

"Never mind about the police department. By we, I mean you, me, Ridge, Chris, Trevor and Ethan. I'll talk to Chris. Maybe he has some room in his case load to look for her, or maybe he knows someone who might," Annabel said. "Ridge works with search and rescue. Maybe he can help."

"Those are good ideas."

Sam's phone rang, and he held up his finger and answered it. He made a few sounds of acknowledgment. Then he disconnected and looked at Annabel.

The expression on his face told her something terrible had happened. "What's wrong?" she asked, dreading the answer.

"There's another body. Another victim of the Alphabet Killer. The chief wants any available officers to lock down the scene. The FBI is on the way. Let's go."

Annabel drove with Sam to the crime scene. A crowd had gathered on the sidewalk. A woman was weeping on the front porch, and another officer was speaking to her.

Sam and Annabel approached, and the other officer took a step away.

"Good morning, ma'am," Sam said.

The woman sniffed and wiped at her eyes. "I came

over to return a pie dish I'd borrowed for a dinner party. She was dead."

"Who is dead?" Annabel asked.

"My friend Henrietta. Henrietta Bell."

An *H* name fit the pattern of the Alphabet Killer.

"Does Henrietta live alone?" Sam asked.

The neighbor shook her head. "She lives with her husband. Their youngest went off to college last year."

Sam pointed to Annabel. "Could you go around the back and make sure no one gets the bright idea to enter the house? I don't want the scene compromised."

Annabel nodded and jogged around the side of the building. She would have liked to listen to the neighbor's answers about the murder, but she was following the chain of command.

"What happened?" a man called to her from a nearby yard.

"We're investigating the report of a crime," Annabel said.

"What crime? A break-in?"

She couldn't answer honestly and openly. "I'm not the detective assigned to the case. I was called in for crowd control. I can't comment further on the situation."

The man muttered something about her being uptight. Annabel ignored it. She had been told to secure the scene, and she would.

As more police and FBI personnel arrived, Annabel remained on the scene to assist as needed. Her connection to Matthew Colton meant she could not handle evidence or write reports about the scene. Her relationship with Jesse made that directive more important.

Regina Willard would be assigned a defense lawyer. Any shred of evidence collected by a Colton would be called into question. Knowing that was a strong incentive to stay away from Jesse. A killer couldn't go free because Annabel hadn't controlled her hormones.

Thinking about letting Jesse go sent blooms of sadness through her. She liked him. Really, really liked him. She didn't usually make connections with people the way she did with Jesse. Her job was important, but despite it only being weeks in the making, her relationship with Jesse was important, too.

She winced when she thought about what had happened the night before. They'd had sex. Amazing sex. They'd connected over a deep-seated issue for both of them. Then she'd panicked and run out. When she was younger, right after her mother had been killed, she had gone to therapy. Annabel mostly recalled being moody and sullen about it. She'd overheard the therapist telling Mama Jean that Annabel would likely struggle with intimacy issues. At the time, Annabel hadn't known or cared what that was, and it had sounded like hocus-pocus. Now, she understood.

A huge leap of faith was required to trust someone with her affections and her heart. She had slept with Jesse, freaked out and fled. A fail for her, and she could only imagine what he was feeling about her.

How could she talk to him about it? What could she say to explain her behavior? She was rude at best, cowardly at the worst. Despite running, Annabel wished she could have another chance with Jesse. She recognized her issues, and she wanted to try again, to do better.

Sam circled the house, a grim expression on his face. Annabel approached. "Are you okay?"

His mouth twitched. "No."

"What's going on?"

"It's not what we thought," Sam said.

Annabel wasn't following. "What isn't?" Was Regina not the killer? Every sign pointed to her, but Annabel didn't have access to the complete evidence on the case.

"There's something off about the crime scene. The FBI is looking into it, but it's missing some of the Alphabet Killer's signatures."

Annabel was intrigued, but she knew better than to question Sam at length about it. "Trevor wants to know if you'll join us at Ethan's place. We want to talk about the alleged Josie sighting."

Annabel felt her temper flare at the word *alleged*. Without the benefit of a good night's sleep and worried about Jesse, her anger boiled over. "Why do you say *alleged*? These are not allegations. I saw Josie. I showed you the charm."

Sam rubbed his jaw. "It seems unlikely. Why would she come to your place, when it's practically condemned? She couldn't have anticipated you would be there."

Annabel prayed she wouldn't hit her brother. It wasn't her way to use fists—she was against violence for many reasons—but he was being dense. "She wouldn't know where else I'd be. And when Ridge said he saw Josie, you believed it. When Lizzie said she saw Josie, you believed it. But when I say that I saw Josie, you act like I'm incapable of recognizing my sister."

"Regina Willard might be in town. If she committed this murder, then she might have been at your place, too. Regina may look vaguely like Josie."

"Since no one knows where Josie is or has a recent picture, then you're right. It could have been Regina. But my instincts tell me the woman on my property this morning was Josie."

"You've been hanging around Jesse Willard. His sister might take exception to that. She might want to know what you're doing with her brother," Sam said.

Annabel set her jaw. "Regina wants to know, or you want to know?"

"Both."

"What I do with my free time is none of your concern," Annabel said, knowing she sounded petulant, but she was tired of being dismissed by her brothers. Nothing she did was right, her personal life was unacceptable to them, and her career choices were rejected.

"It's personal time you're spending with him. It's not just the stakeout?" Sam asked.

He never stopped being a detective. Memories from the night before, locked in Jesse's arms, writhing beneath him, the sensation of him pushing in and out of her, ran through her head, and her body tingled at the memory. "I am handling this."

"Handling it how?" Sam asked.

"I know how to keep my emotions in check. Nothing I do or say to Jesse will pose a threat to the Alphabet Killer case." She was aware she was in a gray area, and she was doing her best to stay on the correct side of it. She was trying not to screw up the Alphabet Killer investigation, and she was trying not to screw up her life and lose the connection to Jesse. He was the first person she had felt this strongly about in her life.

Another detective called to Sam from the doorway.

"I'll see you at Ethan's tonight," Sam said, looking irritated with her.

He was walking away when Annabel realized she hadn't agreed to go to Ethan's. But if she went, she wouldn't let her brothers push her around or make her doubt what she had seen. Josie had been at her house. Annabel was certain of it.

"You're sure it was her?" Trevor asked again. His cherry pie sat untouched in front of him.

Annabel wondered if she should reach across the table and snag it. Eating another piece of pie would take the edge off her annoyance.

Annabel had gone over the details with her brothers three times. Maybe they were hoping she had forgotten something important, like, say, if Josie had left her mailing address and telephone number.

"Annabel already said she was sure of what she

saw," Chris said, rubbing his forehead, appearing frustrated. Annabel appreciated the support from her twin. At least he seemed to believe her without question. Chris wasn't easily duped, and with his PI business, he relied on his instincts.

Annabel took a deep breath and kept her voice even and strong. "It was Josie. If I had any doubts, the charm she left on my porch erased them." Annabel pointed to the charm sitting on the table. She had put it into a plastic bag. She had her charm bracelet with her, too, in case her evidence-driven brothers wanted to compare the two. It had been an ordeal to retrieve her bracelet. Returning to her house was one of her least favorite activities, and rifling through her wet, smelly things was a trial. But she had needed her bracelet to prove the charm wasn't hers. It was the same one their mother had given her and Josie.

Both Sam and Trevor had inspected the charms and the bracelet. They agreed they matched.

"Did she leave anything else?" Ridge asked. "Maybe she dropped something in the yard."

Thinking like a search-and-rescue professional. "We could go over in the daylight and comb the area for anything Josie may have dropped. I still don't understand why she was there," Annabel said, taking a sip of her coffee. It was late to be drinking caffeine, but she was tired and she'd fall asleep easily tonight.

"What time was this?" Sam asked.

Annabel inwardly sighed. "Seven-thirty in the morning."

"What were you doing at your place this morning?" Ethan asked.

This was the part of the story she had glossed over. "I couldn't sleep. I went by the house to take pictures of the damage."

"Were you at Mia's before that?" Ridge asked.

"At that point, yes."

"Where were you earlier?" Trevor asked.

"Out." She didn't want to divert the conversation into one about Jesse. Their problems with Josie were big enough to monopolize the conversation tonight.

Five protective pairs of eyes narrowed on her.

"What does *out* mean?" Sam asked.

"I was in Rosewood."

"You're going to make us drag this out of you," Trevor said.

"If she doesn't want to talk about it, let it go," Chris said.

Annabel smiled appreciatively at her twin. "Thank you, Chris. But if you must know, I've been looking for Dylan Morris."

"Me, too," Trevor, Chris, Ridge, and Sam said at once.

Annabel rolled her eyes. "Then you can't possibly be upset that I was doing the same."

"I can be upset if you were in Rosewood alone, without backup, looking for a criminal," Sam said. "Why didn't you call one of us to go with you? Rosewood has some dicey areas. I don't like the idea of you being without protection."

Annabel hadn't been alone, but saying that was

throwing fuel on the fire. "I know it's hard for everyone to accept, but I am a trained police officer. I'm not an idiot. I don't take unnecessary risks."

"Yet you ran after someone who'd broken into your house, instead of calling for backup," Sam said.

"If I had called for backup, I wouldn't have had a chance to catch her. She wasn't a criminal. It was Josie. Josie wouldn't hurt me."

"Yet she was creeping around your house," Ethan said.

"We don't know what's keeping Josie away. Drugs. Abusive situation. Criminal past," Trevor said.

Annabel wouldn't believe those terrible things about her sister. Trevor was a profiler for the FBI, and he knew too much about how a person became a criminal, the twisted places their minds went that led to a life of crime. He was suspicious of everyone and jumped to the worst-case scenario quickly.

Annabel would keep faith that Josie wasn't in serious trouble. "She hasn't done anything wrong."

"A couple months ago, she was a suspect in an ongoing murder investigation," Sam said.

"We had no proof she had done anything wrong. Everything was circumstantial and guesswork," Annabel said.

"We want you to be safe," Ethan said.

"I will be. But I want us to keep our eyes and ears open. Josie is in town—we don't know why—but she's reached out, however indirectly, three times. If she wants to be part of our lives, I'm more than happy to welcome her," Annabel said.

Her brothers murmured their agreement, and Annabel hoped Josie would visit her again and, maybe, stay and talk.

The Spring Fling had been a Granite Gulch tradition for the past decade. It had started as a high school carnival to raise money for the education system and had morphed into games, food, rides and the sale of produce and specialty items sold by local crafters.

Regina might show at the Spring Fling, possibly hunting for new victims. Every police officer in the Granite Gulch Police Department was working a few shifts during the fling and on high alert to look for anyone matching her description. FBI special agents dressed in plainclothes were positioned in the crowd, searching for any sign of Regina.

Luis was still on medical leave recovering from his injury. Annabel was patrolling alone, although help was close at hand if she needed it.

Annabel stumbled over her feet when she saw a stall for W's Farm. Jesse had decided to abbreviate the name for the Spring Fling, knowing his last name was a problem in town.

Annabel's heart raced, and she considered disappearing deeper into the crowd and avoiding Jesse and his crew entirely. Though she had thought often of what she would say to him, she wasn't prepared, and since she was working, it wasn't an ideal time.

Would there ever be a good time to have an awkward conversation about their relationship? The more time passed, the harder it would be to find solid ground. Annabel moved forward, and as she grew closer, her heart fell.

She had worried about seeing Jesse and his reaction to seeing her. But he wasn't behind the booth. Disappointment took the place of worry. Grace, Tom and a young man, probably Noah, were at the stall.

Annabel was right about Grace being a great face for the farm. She was beautiful and earthy, smiling and looking wholesome, silently beckoning people to purchase their produce. Observing them for a moment, Annabel decided to say hello.

Shoring up her confidence, she stepped in front of the stall. "Everything for sale looks great."

Grace smiled. "Annabel. Welcome. Thank you again for your help with the carriage house. Thanks to some long hours from Tom—" she patted his back affectionately "—and Jesse, the crew and your family, it's almost ready. And not a day too soon for me and Noah." She gave her son a hug around his shoulders, and he shrugged her off.

"Mom, not in front of people," he said.

Grace kissed the top of his head. "Sorry. Forgot the rules for a minute." She rolled her eyes, but they glittered with amusement.

Tom stared at Grace a little long, but quickly caught what he was doing and glanced away.

Annabel read desire in his expression. His long hours on the carriage house made sense.

"Glad to hear it's working out. It will be a great place to live once it's complete," Annabel said.

"I was sorry to hear about your place, too," Grace

said. "Maybe I can return the favor and give you a hand with it?"

Annabel appreciated her thoughtfulness. "The insurance company is making arrangements. It won't be long." Except she had the sense it would be months before she was living at her place.

Grace looked around. "Jesse was here a while ago. I don't know where he disappeared to. I think he's worried about chasing off business if anyone recognizes him."

Grace's tone and words indicated she didn't know what had transpired between Annabel and Jesse. Maybe that was better. Jesse could pretend as though nothing had happened. She and Jesse could return to being a person of interest and a police officer, as if the night they'd spent together didn't exist.

Thinking it made her sad. She couldn't pretend. She didn't have it in her. She had been affected deeply by that night with Jesse, irrevocably changed.

"I should get moving. I'm working today," Annabel said, her uniform making that obvious but feeling awkward about how to walk away.

"Okay, see you around," Grace said with a wave before turning to assist a customer.

She didn't have time to sulk. Annabel had her eyes open for a brunette matching Regina's description, but she was also looking for Josie.

The charm Josie had left on her porch was in her breast pocket. If Josie had kept the charm bracelet all these years, family must mean something to her.

A commotion sounded behind her, and Annabel

turned. Something was happening at W's Farm booth. Annabel rushed through the crowd while calling for backup. The altercation could be nothing, or it could be related to angry townspeople wanting answers about Regina Willard. Or maybe Regina Willard had finally showed herself publicly.

A man was gripping Grace's arm and shaking her. Her son was staring at the man and kicking him. Tom was trying to speak to the man, but he was too busy screaming profanities to hear anyone.

Produce was spilled over the ground. As the first officer on the scene, this was Annabel's situation.

"Police, stop!" Annabel said.

She didn't see a gun in the man's hand. She didn't draw hers. She tried her words again. "Police, put your hands in the air."

Noah stopped kicking the man and faced Annabel.

Out of the corner of her eye, Annabel saw her brother step out of the crowd. Sam was assessing the situation. Keeping her eyes on Grace, Noah, Tom and the attacker in her peripheral vision, she saw Sam point at the child. She nodded discreetly.

"Noah, my brother Sam is standing there. Could you please go with him?"

Annabel wanted Noah out of harm's way, and Sam would keep Noah safe. Drawing her gun when a child was in range terrified her. Too much could go wrong, and an innocent would be harmed. Other officers had responded to her radio call and were moving the crowd farther away.

"Blake is hurting my mom!" Noah said. He was

on the verge of tears, and Annabel didn't blame him. His loyalty to his mother was admirable.

"We'll take care of Blake. Please, go with Detective Sam, and we'll straighten this out."

"Go on, Noah, I'm fine," Grace said, the happiness gone from her eyes, worry in its place.

Noah walked to Sam, looking back at his mom. Annabel felt better knowing one fewer person might be harmed. Tom had his hands in the air, but he hadn't moved away from Grace and Blake. Now, she had to get Grace and Tom away from Blake.

"Blake, can you tell me what's going on?" Annabel asked. She circled and looked for a good position to launch herself at Blake and arrest him. He was bigger than her, but she was smarter.

"She left me. She's pregnant with my baby, and she left me," Blake said, spittle flying from his mouth and his words garbled.

He sounded drunk, and that would make this harder. He was probably irrational, angry and hurt.

Jesse arrived on the scene. Annabel was momentarily distracted but focused on Blake. She wanted him to release Grace before anyone was hurt.

"Hey, man, what's this about?" Jesse asked.

Blake pivoted toward Jesse, and before Blake could answer, Jesse hit him across the face. Blake fell backward into the produce and then slid onto the ground.

Annoyance struck her. She hurried to put the cuffs on Blake and then turned to Jesse. "I was handling this."

"You were. Then I handled it."

Sam walked over and handed Annabel another pair of cuffs. "Arrest him, too."

Annabel blinked at Sam. Jesse had been acting in defense of another, but he had also acted against police orders. Sam outranked her, and there was a crowd. Hating she had to do this, she looked at Jesse. She melted a little and then pulled it together. "Turn around, Jesse."

"Come on, Annabel. I'll come down to the station to talk this out. You don't need the cuffs."

But she did. Sam had told her to arrest him. This was standard operating procedure. With a heavy heart, Annabel screwed her courage up tight and reminded herself this was her job. Her response could set a precedent to the crowd, and she needed the residents of Granite Gulch to respect her. "That's Officer Colton, and don't make me tell you again. Turn around."

Jesse turned and put his hands behind his back. As she clamped the cuffs around Jesse's wrists, Annabel wondered if this was the final knockout blow to their relationship.

Chapter 12

"No! Stop!" Noah's voice broke into Annabel's thoughts, and guilt struck her. Noah rushed to Jesse and threw his arms around his waist. "He didn't do anything. This is Blake's fault. Blake ruins everything."

A torque tightened around Annabel's heart. She hated to do this to Jesse and Noah. Grace looked devastated. Tom appeared miserable. Only Blake seemed to be seething with anger. Where was his guilt and remorse? Annabel wished she had been the one to hit Blake.

Jesse looked at Noah. "I'm fine, buddy. Officer Colton is doing her job. Stay here and look after your mom, okay?"

"I'm coming with you to the station," Grace said.

"I want to make a statement about what happened. You did nothing wrong." She swiveled her gaze and glared at Blake.

Blake swore at her, and Annabel dragged him to his feet. "Shut your mouth, or I'll make this as difficult as possible for you."

With the assistance of several other officers, Annabel drove Blake, and Sam drove Jesse to the police station. Annabel didn't have time to tell Sam to go easy on Jesse or to voice her dissent about Jesse being cuffed.

It certainly wouldn't help his reputation around town, and it wouldn't help their relationship. Blake was ranting in the back of her police cruiser, making it difficult to think, but Annabel wondered what she could say to Jesse to make this right.

Violence against women was intolerable. Jesse had seen his mother battered by her husband and by lousy boyfriends. He had hated it, and when he had been young, he had been too small to stop it. The times he had tried, he had ended up badly beaten, as well. Now, as an adult, and a fairly large one, he had vowed to himself to never, ever knowingly allow a woman in his presence to be harmed.

Seeing Grace manhandled by Blake, and especially while Noah was watching, brought to the surface too many emotions. Though Jesse had seen Detective Colton and Annabel on the scene, he'd felt compelled to act. Jesse would have been wise to keep his hands to himself and let the police handle the situation, but he hadn't been thinking clearly. He had wanted Blake to stop and for Noah and Grace to be physically and emotionally all right.

Sam removed his handcuffs and told him to sit on a bench in the main room near the desks. Jesse could have walked out of the police station, but Sam knew he wouldn't. Jesse wouldn't go on the run over an incident like this. He'd face the music for the choices he'd made, no matter the consequences. If Sam Colton wanted to throw the book at him because he was Regina Willard's brother, then fine. It wouldn't be the first time Jesse had been treated unfairly, and it wouldn't be the last.

Annabel was walking toward the exit of the police station. Seeing her brought back painful memories from the night they'd spent together. She had run out on him, and he wasn't entirely sure what to do with that.

Ignore it? Address it? Pretend what they'd had was meaningless sex? Jesse had had one-night stands before, but they had been in an entirely different context than what he'd experienced with Annabel. He couldn't file those encounters together.

Knowing he was already in trouble, Jesse stood, moving into her path.

Annabel stopped abruptly, avoiding hitting him in the chest. It was reminiscent of the first time they had met. They hadn't exchanged names, but something more powerful had happened in that moment. Here they were again, with miles and hours between them, and it felt as powerful, the connection as strong.

"Hey, Jesse," she said. Her voice was soft and low.

"Hey, you," he said.

She looked around nervously. "I need to get back to the Spring Fling."

"You're not sticking around to deal with this?" he asked.

"Not my domain."

She was running away again. Couldn't she level with him? Wasn't he owed her honesty? "Are you planning to tell me why you left the other night without saying anything?"

Annabel inhaled, as if surprised he had questioned it directly. If he didn't ask the difficult question, he wouldn't have answers. "I have a lot going on in my life right now. I was feeling confused and over-whelmed. Maybe it was a mistake to do what we did."

Her words said one thing, her body language an-other. She leaned toward him, reached to touch his arm and then stopped herself.

"A mistake? It didn't feel like a mistake to me."

Annabel glanced over her shoulder. "After I left, I didn't know what to say to you."

"How about telling me why you left?"

She bit her lip. "It's complicated."

He'd simplify to the heart of the matter. "How much of you leaving had to do with my sister?"

Annabel rubbed her forehead. "Some of it."

That stung. He had thought she was someone whom he could confide in. He had believed she was open-minded and nonjudgmental.

"But not the way you're thinking. I don't think less of you because of who you're related to. Regina is the subject of an active investigation, an investigation I'm supposed to be professional about."

"I see." That had been true since the day they'd met. Why was she making it a problem now? He thought they had crossed this bridge.

"Do you? Because you look angry."

"I'm not angry." He couldn't find the right word to describe what he was feeling. Frustrated? Disappointed?

"We're both going through a lot. Maybe the timing is bad. I don't think you'll be charged for hitting Blake. He deserved it."

She was finished talking about them, and that frustrated him. "Either way, I'll accept whatever punishment is meted out."

"No more fights," Annabel said. "Try to control your temper."

"It wasn't my temper that got the best of me. It was seeing Grace and Noah scared. I can't tolerate that."

Annabel nodded in understanding. "See you around."

"You're running away again," he said, loud enough that several heads turned in their direction.

Annabel stopped, but she didn't face him. Her shoulders sagged, and she hurried out the door of the police precinct.

With a heavy heart, Jesse took a seat on a long bench along the wall and waited for his fate.

* * *

Thanks to the surprising recounting of the situation from Sam Colton, Jesse was released a few hours later. Blake Hernandez had wanted to press charges, but Jesse had been acting in defense of Grace and Noah, and the state had declined to prosecute him.

Jesse was glad to be back on his farm. He was upset about what had happened with Annabel. He sensed she needed space, and he could give her that. When she was ready to talk, if she was ready to talk, he was open to hearing from her.

Tom must have been spending all his spare time preparing the carriage house for Grace and Noah. Grace was moving her things into the house that day, and Jesse was happy she would be close. He could keep an eye on her.

Blake Hernandez was in custody, but Jesse didn't trust that he wouldn't try again to hurt Grace if he was released. Jesse wouldn't let that happen.

Jesse was on his way to the barn. A Granite Gulch Police Department vehicle was parked at the end of his driveway. He ran a frustrated hand over his face. How much more of this could he take? Would the authorities ever leave him alone?

Whistling for his dogs, he waited. They bounded from the barn and came to his side. As he walked, they stayed near him. As he grew closer to the police car, he saw it was occupied by Annabel.

He had come this far, and she had seen him approach, but now he wanted to return to the barn. He'd resolved to give her time and space. His feet had ideas of their own.

When he reached her car, she rolled down the car window. "Hey, Jesse."

Such a casual remark while he was still concealing hurt and anger. "I'm surprised to see you here," Jesse said.

"Surprised?" Annabel asked.

"You hotfooted it out the other night and ran away from me at the precinct. I wouldn't think you'd be back. I figured you needed space. Being at my place is the opposite of space."

She blushed but held his gaze. "I'm working. We're still looking for Regina Willard."

Same old song and dance. "She isn't here," Jesse said.

"I know," Annabel said.

"Then why are you here?" he asked.

"Because it's my job. I was assigned stakeout duty at your farm."

"Why don't you come with me and I'll show you around?" He didn't love the idea of anyone poking around his farm, but he wanted to see Annabel. Maybe he could draw her out and get to the bottom of why she was pulling away from him.

"You're offering to let me look around?" she asked. "I don't have a warrant."

For the opportunity to be with her, he would allow it. "You don't need a warrant because I'm inviting you. Come see what we do here and see I don't have anything to hide," he said.

Annabel climbed out of the car. "Thank you. I would like the tour."

They walked up the driveway. Jesse was proud of what he had accomplished with the farm. He was an open book. If Annabel was worried about him lying to her or being like Regina, she had to see that Jesse was an honest, hardworking man.

As they walked, Annabel asked questions and took her time peering in stalls and behind walls. He didn't let it bother him. He'd expected it.

"I'm sorry about what happened with Blake," Annabel said. "I didn't want to arrest you, but I had no choice."

For a split second, he thought she had been apologizing for sneaking out in the middle of the night. "You were doing your job."

"How are Grace and Noah? Holding it together?" Annabel asked.

"They moved into the carriage house this morning. They had a shockingly small amount of stuff. I'm planning to talk to Noah and get my hands on whatever they might need. Table and chairs, maybe a couch or a television," Jesse said.

"I would offer you a few things, but my personal belongings are smoke-damaged and charred," Annabel said.

"Insurance company helping?" Jesse asked.

"I'm on the wait list for one of their certified renovation teams to work up a few quotes," Annabel said.

"That's good."

Annabel stopped. "Jesse, will you please look at me?"

He pivoted to face her and met her eyes. "What's wrong?"

"We're acting like strangers, and after what we did the other night, we're not strangers. Definitely not," she said, looking him up and down.

When she stared at him with hunger plain in her eyes, he was confused. What did she want from him? No-strings-attached sex? He couldn't give that to her. "No games, Annabel. Tell me what you want." He wouldn't be jerked around, having her change her mind and waffle about what she wanted.

"I'm looking at you this way because I want you."

She launched herself at him, and he caught her in his arms.

Questions flew out of his head. He didn't know the reasons why she was in his arms, but he wouldn't deny her. They had this and it had to be enough.

Whenever Annabel was with Jesse, something switched in her head. They'd had an instant connection from the first time they'd met, and that attraction had grown and changed into more. Everything about Jesse enticed her. He was salt of the earth, a good man who worked hard and looked out for the people he called friends. He was big and strong, and she felt safe with him.

Safe because he wouldn't let anyone hurt her and safe because he didn't care about her past, Matthew Colton's crimes or her connection to a killer. She had been fighting this, trying to convince herself she wasn't good enough. Not being involved with him meant she wouldn't get hurt if it ended. But it hurt not being with Jesse, and that left her with a simple choice: take a chance on happiness or accept the loneliness.

Annabel had complications—the Alphabet Killer investigation, her impending visit with her father, Dylan Morris—and now might not be the best time to start a relationship, but when wasn't life complicated? If she waited until her world was problem free, she would be waiting forever.

She kissed Jesse, threading her fingers through his hair and holding his mouth to hers. His hands went around her waist, and he lifted her. She wrapped her legs around his hips.

He carried her behind a stack of hay inside the barn, next to a pallet of horse feed. "Give me a minute."

He returned with a plaid blanket and spread it on the ground. She crawled on top of it and paused only a moment when she realized she was wearing her police uniform. She was on duty. Crossing into a gray area with Jesse had happened before, and while this was absolutely the most unprofessional thing she had ever done in uniform, she couldn't stop herself.

Jesse took off his hat and set it on the blanket. He covered her body with his. Though it was early in the day, it was already warm outside, cooler in the shade of the barn.

Jesse unbuttoned her shirt, pushing the sides open, and brought his mouth to her breasts. She was wearing a plain white bra, but he stared at her and she felt like a swimsuit model on a photo shoot.

He moved lower to her belt, unfastening it. She reached to his and did the same. Sliding out of his pants, he kicked them off. He removed her pants and underwear at once, and she parted her legs, wanting him, welcoming him.

"Please, hurry," she said.

The possibility of being caught and that this was utterly forbidden had her heart slamming hard and heat smoldering through her.

Jesse grabbed his jeans, pulling his wallet from the pocket and removing a condom. She snatched it from his hand.

"Let me." She tore it open and rolled it on, tossing the wrapper over her head.

Jesse shifted to align their bodies. Their eyes connected, and he pushed inside her. She felt his fierce need to take her, dominate her. Maybe he was harboring some anger from how she had left the other night, but she didn't question it now. This was moving them in the direction of making it right between them.

He moved rapidly inside her, and she couldn't get enough. Her ponytail was rubbing against the blanket. She removed the elastic holding her hair.

Relaxing into the sensations that washed over her, she lifted her hips into his, unable to do anything except feel.

Then he stopped, holding her close and flipping onto his back, their bodies still joined.

She adjusted her legs, bracing her knees against

the ground and setting her hand on his chest for leverage. He massaged her bare breasts with his hands,
and she rode him hard, pushing her hips against his.
Bouncing wildly on him, she felt the tightening of her
body, and she convulsed, pleasure washing over her.

She let her orgasm pulse over her, and Jesse joined
her. Annabel rolled to the side and lay on the blanket, sweat covering her body, her muscles relaxed.

"Want a shower?" he asked.

Her hair was sticking to her back. A shower might
be a good idea. "Sure. Race you?"

They scrambled to pull on their clothes, Annabel
giving Jesse a playful shove to knock him over and
get a head start to the house.

"Were you listening to the radio today?" Sam
asked.

Annabel jolted. She had been lost in thought about
Jesse, picturing his handsome face, his muscled body,
and reliving her entirely inappropriate romp in the
hay with him. "What? The radio?"

Sam gave her a strange look. "While on stakeout.
Gets pretty boring. I didn't know if you'd heard about
Henrietta Bell."

The Coltons were gathered at Ethan's place again.
It was a rare evening when Sam and Zoe, Ethan and
Lizzie, Ridge and Darcy, and Annabel, Chris and
Trevor were free for dessert.

Annabel shook her head. "What about her?"

Trevor set a pitcher of lemonade on the table.
"Turns out, she's not the Alphabet Killer's latest

victim. The GGPD released a statement today. Her husband is missing and is being charged with her murder."

"Is her husband suspected of being involved with the Alphabet Killer?" Chris asked, pouring himself a glass of lemonade.

Lizzie had baked a layer cake with meringue buttercream frosting. She had made the extra effort to tint each layer. When the cake was cut, it was a rainbow of colors.

"As far as we know, the husband used what he could gather about the Alphabet Killer from the news to copycat the technique. He was hoping to have the murder pinned on the Alphabet Killer, and he could go free," Trevor said.

Annabel hadn't heard. "That's awful. I'm sorry to hear it."

"We don't have any recent leads to track the killer," Sam said.

"How's the stakeouts at the Willard's Farm been going?" Ridge asked. "It must get tiring out there, watching crops grow for hours."

Annabel felt her face growing hot. She busied herself pouring more lemonade into her cup. Too bad it wasn't wine. She might need it to get through this evening. "Not really. Today, Jesse asked if I wanted to look around the farm."

"Did you?" Trevor asked.

"Yes, and I didn't see any signs of the Alphabet Killer," she said.

Her brothers exchanged looks. Was she acting funny? "What's the matter?" she asked.

"You're spending a lot of time with Jesse Willard," Chris said.

"I've been assigned stakeouts at this house," Annabel said.

"Is that the extent of it?" Trevor asked.

"Usually, police officers don't fraternize with the subject of a stakeout," Sam said.

She didn't want to be profiled and her actions scrutinized. "Don't dig around my psyche. Jesse has become a friend. Someone I trust."

"Trust?" Sam asked.

"He protected me when someone took shots at me. And most of you have met him. Didn't you like him?"

The members of her family, with the exception of Sam, nodded their heads in agreement.

"Then why the questions?" Annabel asked, trying to stay calm. Talking about Jesse riled her up, and when she and her brothers discussed these topics, she felt attacked. "When each of you met your significant others, I didn't ask questions. I was happy that you seemed happy. Why can't I get the same respect?"

"Are you saying you've fallen for him?" Darcy asked.

Annabel didn't know how to answer that question. That had been the implication in her statement, but she hadn't meant to reveal so much. She and Jesse were working on their relationship, and Annabel had high hopes. "I like him. It's complicated because of who his sister is. She's involved in an important case, and it's difficult to have a close relationship with Jesse right now because of that." As she said the words, she felt an ache in her chest. She hadn't spoken aloud about her feelings for Jesse before, and now that she had outwardly acknowledged the barrier between them, she knew they were unavoidable.

Silence filled the room.

"You aren't technically assigned to the Alphabet Killer case," Sam said.

Stunned her brother would look for loopholes for her, her gaze swerved to him. "Meaning?"

"Meaning, Chief Murray is trying to keep us out of the investigation to the greatest degree possible, and I don't see the big deal if you tell the chief you're now invested in the case in another way," Sam said.

"I would think hiding it would be the problem," Chris said. "If you put it in the open, then it can't bite you later."

"Makes sense to me," Ridge said.

Trevor nodded his agreement.

"Are you telling me you are okay with me seeing Jesse Willard?" Annabel asked.

Darcy, Lizzie and Zoe voiced their agreement enthusiastically and her brothers a bit less excitedly.

"We'll still worry," Trevor said.

"And be overprotective," Chris said.

"But we want you to be happy," Ridge said. "I met the guy. He seemed decent."

Not over-the-top praise, but from her brothers, it was amazing to hear. Emotion tightened her throat.

"Your support means a lot to me. Thanks, guys. It makes it easier to think."

"It's good that you can think, because you're scheduled to see Matthew soon, and you need to bring your A game," Trevor said. "He'll try to mess with you. He's had time to look for ways to screw with you."

Thinking about seeing her father made her feel ill. One visit per child per month, and she was up next. She expected the worst. "I'll remember everything he says and repeat it to you guys. Maybe we can read between the lines and find out what he did with our mother."

Silence fell around the room as was often the case when their mother was mentioned.

"I hope I can pull more from Matthew than a one-word clue," Annabel said.

"Good luck with that," Sam said.

"He is tough to crack. I wanted to crack his head. He seemed delighted that I wanted to know more and that he wouldn't tell me," Ridge said.

"Delighted or just out-of-his-mind crazy? Because he seemed crazy to me," Ethan said. Lizzie patted Ethan's hand.

"Both," Annabel said. She was prepared to face whatever Matthew was handing out. One skill she had learned while in foster care was how to stuff her emotions under a mask of indifference and how to control her reactions. "I can deal with Matthew. I can't think of anything he would say to me that would shake me. I've read it all. I've thought it all."

"He's a twisted man, Annabel. We may have written him off, but he's made it his business to know about us. He'll know how to get into your head and which buttons to push," Trevor said.

"I'll be ready for him." Getting her clue from Matthew about the location of their mother's body would close that chapter of her life, and she was more than ready to say good riddance to Matthew Colton.

Chapter 13

Annabel pulled up to Willard's Farm. This would be her last day on stakeout. Luis was returning from medical leave at the end of the week, and Annabel was mentally composing her speech on how she would inform Chief Murray that watching Jesse Willard's farm was a conflict of interest. She couldn't be objective about Jesse anymore.

Annabel wouldn't help Jesse hide Regina, but she also didn't believe he was knowingly concealing her. Though Chief Murray might ask uncomfortable questions, Annabel was prepared to answer them honestly. Well, mostly honestly.

She wouldn't get into details about their between-the-sheets activities.

She needed to talk with Jesse. Telling him her revelation was best done in person. Though she wasn't sure how he would respond, she'd tell him that she liked him. Liked him and wanted to move forward with their relationship. No meaningless quickies in the barn and no running out in the middle of the night. She was in this, wholeheartedly.

She climbed out of the car and walked up Jesse's driveway. How would she start the conversation? What could she say to explain how she felt?

Striding to the front door, Annabel took a deep breath and knocked. Silence. She turned, looking around the farm. Jesse might not be home. He could be working in the fields. Feeling disappointed that her conversation would have to wait, she rang the doorbell, in case he was inside and hadn't heard her.

She noticed the door was not latched tight, and her heart pounded. Was Jesse inside? Had he forgotten to pull the door closed?

Taking her gun in her hand, she radioed for backup. She might be overreacting, or Regina Willard might be on the other side of the door.

She pushed the door open with her foot. "Jesse?"

No response. She looked around the corner, raising her gun.

Her heart was roaring loudly, and it was hard to hear. She didn't need an explanation for what was happening in front of her.

Dylan Morris was holding Jesse at gunpoint. Jesse was seated on the couch, and Dylan retreated a few steps, holding his gun between Jesse and her.

"Glad you came in. I told him to call for you. Like

a good boyfriend, he refused. Didn't want to put you in danger," Dylan said.

If Dylan hurt Jesse, Annabel would kill him. That instinct knocked her off-kilter. She hadn't felt the urge to harm someone as much as she felt it now when Jesse's life was threatened. "This has nothing to do with him, Dylan. Let him go."

Dylan laughed. "After what you put me through, you are in no position to ask for favors."

What she had done? He was the criminal on the run. "Okay, Dylan. Let's stay calm and talk about this."

"I want you to stop following me. Stop stalking me. Stop sending your cop family after me. I want to live my life. I want to enjoy my life. I don't want to be hounded everywhere I go. Your house blew up, and you still didn't take the hint," Dylan said.

He had implicated himself in setting the bomb at her house. Anger coiled around her, sharpening her senses and her thoughts. Dylan seemed oblivious to the fact that he had committed a crime and was a wanted man. She didn't have the power to stop the Granite Gulch Police Department from looking for him. Her interest in him wasn't personal. "I understand. The situation is tough. You need to let Jesse leave, and then we can talk."

Dylan looked from Jesse to Annabel. "He should stay."

"Then let's put away our weapons. Shooting a cop won't get the GGPD off your tail. That will bring every cop in Texas looking for you," Annabel said.

Sweat dripped from Dylan's forehead. "Stop talking for a second, so I can think." He wiped at his face. "Why is it hot in here?" He looked around, and his gun lowered slightly.

Jesse launched himself from the couch and tackled Dylan. The gun went off. Jesse grabbed Dylan's arm, pinning it above his head. Annabel stepped on Dylan's arm until he released the gun. She removed it from his reach.

"Dylan Morris, you're under arrest." Annabel took great delight in listing his crimes. Jesse rolled him over, and Annabel handcuffed him.

She and Jesse dragged Dylan to his feet.

As they marched him down the driveway, Annabel heard the approach of police sirens.

"He was waiting in my kitchen when I came inside," Jesse said. "I came in the back door. He must have used the front."

"I'm glad you're okay," Annabel said.

"Were you here for another stakeout?" Jesse asked.

"Yes."

"Why were you coming to the house?" Jesse asked.

Annabel took a deep breath. "Let's get Dylan in the car, and we'll talk."

When they arrived at her police car, Annabel put Dylan in the backseat. She turned on the engine, letting the air-conditioning blow, and closed the door, locking him in.

She wouldn't take chances of an escape by cracking the window.

"I was at Ethan's last night. My brothers were

with their significant others. At least, Sam, Ethan and Ridge were. They seemed happy. I was jealous."

"Jealous of what?"

"They've found someone to spend their lives with. Someone who accepts them and cares for them and wants to be with them. They go home and have someone waiting for them. They can build a life and a home of their dreams and share it with someone who cares about them."

Annabel took a deep breath. "Seeing them made me miss you. I'd been trying to keep you in a box, in a safe place, like you were some guy I was having a good time with. But you're more than that to me."

As the police pulled up to the car, Annabel wished she could have five more minutes. Sam and Trevor exited their car and jogged to their sister.

"Are you okay?" Sam asked.

"I'm fine. Dylan Morris was holding Jesse hostage. We worked together to stop him."

Sam extended his hand to Jesse. They shook hands. "Thank you, Jesse. Thank you for looking out for our sister."

"Annabel's a good cop. She handled Dylan like a pro," Jesse said.

The unexpected praise made her blush. "I did what I was trained to do," Annabel said.

"You've impressed people, Annabel," Trevor said. "I've been busy, but I've noticed how you've handled yourself in the field."

"The chief has noticed it, too," Sam said.

"Ready to take in your collar? The second most wanted person in Granite Gulch?" Trevor asked.

Annabel looked at Jesse. She had more to say, but it would have to wait. She didn't want to talk about her feelings for him in front of her brothers. "Jesse, I'll talk to you soon?"

He nodded. "Sure. I'm guessing I'll need to give a statement to the police."

She hadn't meant him discussing his statement. She wanted to finish their personal conversation. No way was she saying that to Jesse in front of her brothers.

She climbed in the car, and Sam slid in the passenger seat. "You're letting me drive?" she asked.

Sam smiled at her, pride obvious on his face. "Your collar. I'm here to assist."

Her brothers were finally accepting her as their colleague, and it meant the world to her, but she couldn't stop thinking about Jesse. They had much to discuss.

Annabel was greeted like a hero at the police precinct. Her fellow officers and detectives nodded their approval, patting her on the back. She hadn't before felt like such a part of the team.

Dylan Morris was booked and was taken to questioning. He was smart enough to ask for a lawyer, but Annabel knew he would be charged with a variety of crimes.

"Ethan and Lizzie are making dinner to celebrate. You coming?" Sam asked.

She wanted to return to Willard's Farm to talk to Jesse, but her family was celebrating her, her accomplishment. Bigger, her accomplishment as a police officer. How could she say she had other plans?

"That sounds great," Annabel said. "I'll call Lizzie and let her know I'm coming and see what I can bring." It didn't seem fair to infringe on Lizzie's hospitality again, especially when she was pregnant. She appeared to enjoy being the hostess. Annabel couldn't offer for the family to come to her burned-out shell of a house.

That evening, Annabel walked into Ethan and Lizzie's place carrying a tray of fruit she'd picked up from the grocery store. The greeting she received from her siblings and their significant others and her friend Mia was overwhelming. Annabel set the fruit on the table and felt herself getting choked up.

Mia hugged her. "You caught him. That's amazing."

Annabel brushed her hair away. "It's not like I caught the Alphabet Killer."

"It's still great," Chris said. "I feel better knowing he's off the streets."

Annabel did, too. "I have other good news. On the drive over, I received a call from my home insurance company. They've approved the claim on the house, and renovations start in two weeks."

Her family cheered.

"I have great news, too," Sam said. Annabel looked at Zoe, expecting the news involved her. Sam rolled his eyes. "Not that kind of good news. We searched

Dylan Morris's girlfriend's apartment. We found the supplies used to build the bomb that was set at your house and located seven firearms. One of them is a match to the gun used in the shooting at Willard's Farm. Ballistics will confirm it's a match, but my gut tells me the guy is guilty as sin."

Relief rushed over her knowing the Alphabet Killer hadn't been taking aim at her or Jesse. Dylan Morris was in custody, and with the mounting evidence, he would be in prison for a long time.

Mia thrust a glass of wine into Annabel's hand. "To Annabel and the successful prosecution of that scumbag Dylan Morris. May he rot in prison and never hurt anyone again!"

Her family raised their glasses, and then Ridge prompted her. "Say something, Annabel. What's on your mind?"

She had one prevailing thought. "I wish Jesse were here."

Annabel sat across from Chief Murray. Her palms were sweaty, but she had to tell him about her and Jesse.

"Chief, I asked to speak with you today to let you know I've formed a friendship with Jesse Willard. Spending time with him, I don't think I can be objective about the case."

Chief Murray stared at her for an eternity. Was he thinking about disciplining her? Putting her back on the information desk? Firing her?

"That's timely. If Regina Willard is planning to

hide at Willard's Farm, she is smart enough to avoid the cops. It's not a good use of your or anyone else's time to stake out the farm. I'm arranging for the entire department to do occasional sweeps, in case she shows up and for the safety of Jesse Willard and his staff. But we need to focus on other leads."

Her shoulders relaxed. She wasn't in trouble.

"I've been pleased with the way you've handled yourself in the field, and I want to see you take on more responsibilities. Luis is returning in a couple of days. He's an experienced cop, and you two make a good team. I plan to give you more challenging assignments. Of course, I'll still need someone to help Mrs. Granger and Cubbles, but that won't be your full-time job."

"Thanks, Chief," Annabel said. The prospect of helping Mrs. Granger find her cat a couple times a week didn't seem as bad, knowing she would have other interesting cases to work on.

"Dismissed."

Annabel saluted and stood, hurrying from the office. It had gone better than she had hoped.

Now, she needed to talk to Jesse. She called his cell phone and left him a voice mail, asking him to call her as soon as he received the message. Then she waited.

Annabel was not prepared to face her father. She had thought she was. She had believed that she was emotionally capable of seeing him. But now, thinking of the long drive to the prison and what awaited her, she wanted to back out. Ask someone else to go for her. Would her father know who she was? Would her father recognize her?

How much information had Matthew collected on her and her siblings over the years? She believed he didn't care about them, and that was easier for her to accept than to consider that he did care, that he had made a terrible mistake and regretted it. All criminals regretted being caught. Few regretted their actions.

Jesse hadn't returned her calls. After visiting her father, she would go see him. Seeing her father would emotionally exhaust her and likely try her patience. Jesse would restore her. Being with Jesse made her feel whole and strong and capable.

Annabel was wearing comfortable clothes. She wasn't dressing up for her father. He wanted to see his children before he died. He would see her. Could she sit across from him, the bulletproof glass between them, and say nothing, except to demand her clue? Would he try to antagonize her?

She had questions for her father, but she would not ask them. He was incapable of answering them in a manner that was satisfactory. Why give him the pleasure of lording something else over her?

Matthew Colton was dying. These were his last days on earth. Had anything changed? How would she feel when he was dead? Her father had been lost to her years before from the moment he had gone on a murder spree, killing individuals who reminded him of his brother. What she had left was Matthew Colton, like a cruel joke life had played on her, leaving a sick, twisted, bitter man in place of the father she would have liked to have.

Mia was at work. She had offered to stay home with Annabel or to drive with her to the prison, but Annabel could do this. She wanted to prove to herself she was strong enough.

She left the house, checking that she had her keys, phone and badge. She didn't need her badge, but it was a safety blanket. Though she wouldn't be so bold, she would have liked to slam it against the glass and show her father that he had created another police officer. She was on the team of people who found and arrested people like her father.

She froze on the sidewalk. Jesse was parked in front of Mia's place, leaning against his car. All six foot something of his delicious cowboy self, clad in jeans and plaid, his Stetson resting on his head. He removed his hat as she approached.

"What are you doing here?" she asked.

"Came to town for church service. Tom proposed to Grace right after, and she accepted."

"That's great news," Annabel said.

"I'm happy for Tom and Grace, but I've been thinking of you. I didn't plan to come here, but my car had a mind of its own," he said.

"I've been calling you."

Jesse slipped his thumbs into his pants pockets, and Annabel's lust hummed louder. "I needed time to figure out what I wanted to say to you."

"Did you figure it out?" she asked, knowing she might not like his response. Given that she was about to face an emotionally challenging day with Matthew Colton, she should have put Jesse off. But it seemed as if they had been put off too many times and their relationship was too fragile to handle more distance.

"I don't like dancing around my feelings for you. I don't like going to sleep with you beside me and waking alone. If we're going to do this, then we're going to do it. I want to do this. I want you, and I have from the first moment I saw you."

Her heart leaped with joy. He wanted to be with her. "I told my boss I couldn't do any more stakeouts at your farm because we were involved."

He arched a brow. "How'd he handle that?"

"He accepted it. The chief isn't planning any more surveillance at your farm. We'll have police cruisers driving by to ensure your safety, but no one believes you're guilty."

"Then you're not involved in looking for my sister?" Jesse asked.

"No more than any other officer," she said. They were touching on a delicate topic, but both of them were handling it well. It was welcome progress in their relationship. If they were going to be together, they'd have to face these issues. "As far as the GGPD and I are concerned, I can do this, and it's not a problem." She closed the distance between them and slipped her arms around his neck, lacing her fingers. She brought his mouth down on hers in a deep, soul-shaking kiss.

Her mouth coaxed his open, and then her tongue was sliding against his, dueling, tangling. His arms banded around her waist, his hat tapping the back of her thighs.

He broke the kiss. "How about we take this some-where more private? This might be aboveboard, but I'd like my lady to maintain her reputation in town."

She laughed. "Your lady?"

"I'd like to give you another name."

She lifted her brow in question.

"My wife." He pulled a ring from his jeans pocket. "This is the ring Frank gave my mother. It changed our lives for the better. I hope it does the same for us. Annabel Colton, will you marry me?" He kissed her then, a quick kiss on the mouth.

Emotion swelled inside, and her heart clamored with an immediate response. "Yes, Jesse, I'll marry you."

She was prepared to take his hand and follow him wherever he wanted to go, but then reality came down on her hard. "I would love to spend the rest of the day with you, but I have an appointment."

"With your father." He must have heard the heavy sadness in her voice.

"With my father."

"I'll drive you," he said.

"I can handle it."

Jesse frowned. "Don't start that again. We made it official. We're a couple, and that means I'm here for you, like I know you'll be here for me when Regina turns up."

When Regina was brought to justice, Annabel

didn't want him facing that alone and feeling as if he needed to shut her out. "We'll do this together."

He took her hand and squeezed it, bringing it to his mouth and kissing the back of it. "Together."

Chapter 14

Annabel sat in the cracked plastic orange chair and waited for her father to be brought to the other side of the window. The prison smelled like sweat and bleach, a combination that nauseated her.

She had the ring Jesse had given her tucked in her pocket, along with the charm Josie had left on her porch.

The moment Matthew appeared, she knew it was him. Wearing an orange jumpsuit, his hands and feet shackled, he looked frail.

He lifted his head to meet her gaze. There was nothing frail in his expression. It took everything she had to stay in her chair. She wanted to turn and run. Her siblings were counting on her.

Matthew shuffled to the chair on his side of the

window and sat. He reached for the phone and held it to his ear.

Annabel did the same.

Neither said anything for a long time.

"Officer Colton, it is a pleasure to see you."

He knew she was a cop. Good. She was firmly on the side of the law, and she detested what he had done. She wasn't a crazy fanatic coming to praise him for his supposed criminal genius. "What is my clue?" she asked. She was here. Those were the terms. Show up. Get clue. Leave.

"I imagined you would look like your mother."

The woman he had murdered in cold blood? Annabel was tempted to snap at him, make a cutting remark and be unpleasant, but he wanted that. He was goading her. He had manipulated his children to show up, and it was enough of a coup.

"My clue?" Annabel asked.

"Have you and your brothers figured it out yet?" Matthew asked.

She was tired of repeating herself.

"It's simple. You should have figured it out by now. That you don't know tells me you're still emotionally involved and not seeing clearly. I find that satisfying. Almost as satisfying that you finally became a cop. Did you enjoy reading my letters from Regina Willard?"

Annabel bit her tongue so hard she thought she might bite it off. "Where is Regina?"

Matthew smiled, and Annabel berated herself for engaging him in this ridiculous conversation. She didn't want to be here. Jesse was waiting on the far side of the room for her signal to move closer if she needed him. The guard who had cleared her visit had extended her a professional courtesy to allow Jesse to stay with her.

"I don't know where Regina is. She hasn't written me. I miss her letters. How sad for me."

"There are a lot of things sad about you." She felt the words bubbling inside her, and she figured, why not let them out? He couldn't hurt her anymore. "You gave up your wife and children for what? Some deranged killing spree? Whatever your brother did that made you unable to cope, you should think about the fact that you're in prison. Think about why your brother could manipulate you easily."

Matthew's eyes flared with anger. "My little Annabel, is that how you speak to your father?"

"I have no father. Now tell me my clue."

"Why are you eager to cut short our visit?"

"I am here for my clue."

"I have a club of devoted fans. What if I sent a few of them after you? Or Josie? Would that get your attention?"

Annabel controlled her anger. He didn't have that power. "Where is Josie?"

Matthew shrugged. "I could find her."

He was bluffing. If Chris couldn't locate her, no way could a band of unhinged psycho-worshippers find her. "I carry a gun. So, please, send someone after me. I shoot to kill."

He laughed. "Annabel, you are a delight. I wouldn't

want to hurt my children. I tried to help you when they took you from me."

Again, she was taken from her family because Matthew had killed their mother. The cancer medication must be affecting his brain.

"Are you planning to invite your boyfriend over to chat, or is he for show?" Matthew asked.

How had he known Jesse was with her? Jesse must have looked in her direction once too often.

"If he comes over, I'll give you your clue. It will be a nice rite of passage for you, letting your father meet and approve of your boyfriend."

Annabel was disgusted by the idea. Matthew's approval meant nothing. But if meeting Jesse hastened this disturbing conversation, she was on board. She motioned for Jesse, and he swaggered over.

Matthew clapped his hands in delight, a difficult feat in cuffs. "Regina Willard's brother. I suppose I will take credit for your happiness then. I am pleased that you and Jesse have met and gotten on well. Regina is a delight. I can only imagine what her brother is like."

Annabel felt her defensiveness of Jesse rise. "You get some sick pleasure sitting in prison trying to manipulate people who want nothing to do with you. I am here to find out where Mom is buried. That's it. Get this through your head. Jesse is nothing like Regina. I won't tell you how wonderful he is, because you don't get to know him. You don't get to be part of my life or Sam's, Ethan's, Chris's, Ridge's, Trevor's or Josie's, because you gave up that right. We're doing great things, and instead of being part of that, you're in prison. Now give me my clue."

He looked at her for a long time. Annabel would wait him out if she had to.

"Peaches."

"Peaches?" Annabel repeated, wanting to make sure she heard him.

Matthew nodded.

"Tell me where mom is, and I will tell you something about my life. Something you might enjoy," Annabel said.

Matthew leaned closer as if considering it. "That wasn't the deal. One clue each. If I tell you more, then Chris and Trevor won't come see me."

Matthew disgusted her. "Goodbye, Matthew. May God have mercy on your soul." Annabel slammed down the phone. Jesse wrapped his arm around her shoulders, and together, they left the prison.

Epilogue

"Peaches?" Zoe asked, adjusting her glasses and adding the word to her notes. She was researching the word in connection with the others: *Texas*, *hill*, *B* and now *peaches*.

"Mom's parents had a place in Bearson, Texas," Trevor said. "It was on a hill on a huge spread of land."

"What about peaches?" Ethan asked.

"They had peach trees in the backyard," Trevor said.

"Do you think Matthew would have buried Mom at her parents' place?" Sam asked.

Annabel didn't know what to make of the clues. Matthew could be jerking them around and leading them nowhere. Why would he do something almost nice for the woman he'd murdered? Annabel leaned against Jesse, happy to have him close, needing his support and love.

"We could visit the house," Ridge said.

"The property belongs to us, and it wouldn't hurt to visit," Sam said.

Except it did hurt. Emotionally, none of them wanted to face that lost part of their past. They had each visited the Bearson house a few times, but it seemed to leave a press of sadness on them when they went. They didn't stay long. "Maybe if we dig around the peach trees, we'll find Mom," Annabel said.

"Or we could dig up the entire property," Sam said. "How do we know which peach tree?"

"The original investigation into Mom's disappearance included cadaver dogs," Ridge said. "No remains were found."

Annabel didn't have answers, but she knew they'd need more clues. The amount of resources it would require to dig up the entire Bearson property looking for their mother would be extensive and take too much time. They couldn't accomplish it fast enough to save Chris and Trevor from visiting Matthew.

If they wanted closure on the past, they'd each have to visit with their serial-killer father. At least, come what may, Jesse would be at her side. Annabel had found love in the most unexpected place, and she would fight to keep it.

* * * * *

*Don't miss the next book in
the thrilling* COLTONS OF TEXAS *series,
HER COLTON P.I., by Amelia Autin,
available May 2016
from Harlequin Romantic Suspense.*

*And if you loved this novel, be sure to check out
other titles by C.J. Miller:*

*GUARDING HIS ROYAL BRIDE
THE SECRET KING
CAPTURING THE HUNTSMAN
TAKEN BY THE CON
COLTON HOLIDAY LOCKDOWN
UNDER THE SHEIK'S PROTECTION
TRAITOROUS ATTRACTION
PROTECTING HIS PRINCESS
SHIELDING THE SUSPECT
HIDING HIS WITNESS*

*Available now from
Harlequin Romantic Suspense!*

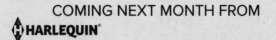
#1895 CONARD COUNTY SPY
Conard County: The Next Generation
by Rachel Lee
On the run from danger, ex–CIA agent Trace Archer
seeks help in Conard County, Wyoming, from a former
colleague. But when beautiful teacher Julie Ardlow offers
him protection, danger and desire combine to create an
incredibly potent mixture.

#1896 HER COLTON P.I.
The Coltons of Texas
by Amelia Autin
As danger threatens Blackthorn County, Texas, private
investigator Chris Colton takes on his hardest assignment yet:
protecting Holly McCay and her twins. But it's Chris's heart
that's really at risk!

#1897 DEADLY OBSESSION
by Elle James
Suffering from PTSD, former army ranger Chance McCall
jumps at the opportunity to visit coastal Cape Churn for a
friend's wedding, where he meets Jillian Taylor. As he helps
the ravishing real estate agent solve the mystery of a haunted
house, he soon realizes he might be the next down the aisle.

#1898 BODYGUARD'S BABY SURPRISE
Bachelor Bodyguards
by Lisa Childs
To protect the woman he inadvertently put in danger,
FBI Special Agent Nicholas Rus becomes a bodyguard to
girl-next-door Annalise Huxton. Now that she's carrying his
child, no threat will keep him from her—or their family.

HRSCNM0416

REQUEST YOUR FREE BOOKS!
2 FREE NOVELS PLUS 2 FREE GIFTS!

⊕ HARLEQUIN®

ROMANTIC suspense

Sparked by danger, fueled by passion

HRS15

She didn't want to do it, but Chris's points were irrefutable. She suddenly realized her palms were damp, and she rubbed them nervously on the sides of her jeans. "So when do we start?"

"As soon as I can coordinate things with Sam and Annabel—tomorrow or the next day. And I've got to get Jim Murray's blessing, too." She raised her brows in a question, and he added, "He's the Granite Gulch police chief. Sam and Annabel answer to him, so we can't do this without him giving it the green light. But I don't see Jim saying no."

"Can he be trusted?" Holly blurted out.

Chris smiled faintly. "He's honest as the day is long. I've known him since I was a kid, and I would trust him to do the right thing. Always."

"Okay," she said again. She didn't say anything more, but she didn't leave, either. She knew she should—that would be the safe thing. The smart thing. But suddenly all she could think of was the kiss in her dream yesterday. The kiss that had devastated her with how much she wanted this man she barely knew. And then there was the kiss that wasn't. The almost-kiss in the kitchen last night. She'd seen it in his eyes—he'd wanted to kiss her. Why hadn't he?

Then she realized he was looking at her the same way he had last night, as if he was a little boy standing on the sidewalk outside a store window gazing longingly at something he wanted but knew he couldn't have because he couldn't afford it. As if—

"Go to bed, Holly," he told her, his voice suddenly harsh. But she couldn't seem to make her feet move. "This isn't what you want." Oh, but it was, it *was*.